Drug Lords 2

Lock Down Publications and Ca$h Presents

Drug Lords 2

A Novel by *Ghost*

Drug Lords 2

Lock Down Publications
P.O. Box 870494
Mesquite, Tx 75187

Visit our website @
www.lockdownpublications.com

Copyright 2020 by Ghost
Drug Lords 2

First Edition January 2020
Printed in the United States of America

Lock Down Publications
Like our page on Facebook: Lock Down Publications @
www.facebook.com/lockdownpublications.ldp
Cover design and layout by: **Dynasty Cover Me**
Book interior design by: **Shawn Walker**
Edited by: **Sunny Giovanni**

Stay Connected with Us!

Text **LOCKDOWN** to 22828 to stay up-to-date with new releases, sneak peaks, contests and more…

Thank you.

Submission Guideline.

Submit the first three chapters of your completed manuscript to ldpsubmissions@gmail.com, subject line: Your book's title. The manuscript must be in a .doc file and sent as an attachment. Document should be in Times New Roman, double spaced and in size 12 font. Also, provide your synopsis and full contact information. If sending multiple submissions, they must each be in a separate email.

Have a story but no way to send it electronically? You can still submit to LDP/Ca$h Presents. Send in the first three chapters, written or typed, of your completed manuscript to:

LDP: Submissions Dept
Po Box 870494
Mesquite, Tx 75187

DO NOT send original manuscript. Must be a duplicate.

Provide your synopsis and a cover letter containing your full contact information.

Only if your submission is **approved**, will you then get a response letter.

Thanks for considering LDP and Ca$h Presents.

Dedications:

First of all, this book is dedicated to my Baby Girl 3/10, the love of my life and purpose for everything I do. As long as I'm alive, you'll never want nor NEED for anything. We done went from flipping birds to flipping books. The best is yet to come.

To LDP'S CEO- Ca$h & COO- Shawn:

I would like to thank y'all for this opportunity. The wisdom, motivation, and encouragement that I've received from you two is greatly appreciated.

The grind is real. The loyalty in this family is real. I'm riding with LDP 'til the wheels fall off.

THE GAME IS OURS!

I GOT THE STREETS!

Ghost

Drug Lords 2

Chapter 1

That night, JaMichael woke Makaroni up at three o'clock in the morning with an assault rifle in his hand. He was breathing hard. He had a mug on his face. "Say, lil' cuz, I need you to roll out to Orange Mound wit' me so we can holler at these Duffel Bag Cartel niggas. They acting like they don't wanna fall in line. But I got a plan for all of that." He slammed a magazine into his Choppah and cocked it.

Stevo stepped beside him with a grim look on his face. "Mack, get yo ass up so we can go over here and holler at these niggas. JaMichael say that if we ride wit' him tonight that he'll give us ten gees a piece and that it ain't got nothin' to do wit' that Rebirth that we leaving wit'."

"Yeah, lil' homie, I know ten bands ain't a whole lot of money but it's somethin'. Besides, I don't think we gon' have to do much anyway. But in case we do, I know for sure I'll have two Hittas beside me."

Makaroni sat on the edge of the bed. He was more tired than he had ever been before. Jahliya had really worn him out. "Damn, when y'all trying to do all of this?" He yawned.

"Right now. We need to holler at Phoenix n'em like ASAP. That nigga just heard that I've bought up the main property in the Orange Mound where he and his Duffel Bag Cartel crew are operating, and he's insisting that he and I meet face to face to determine how shit is about to go down from here on out. I don't like Phoenix. That nigga is real shysty to me. I don't care if we share the same blood or not."

"Wait, you saying that this nigga is supposed to be some kin to us?" Makaroni asked, before yawning again.

"Yeah, he family. Real distant though. Like a third cousin a somethin'. Anyways, fuck that fool. When it comes to the money, all that family shit is out of the window. Blood don't

fund my lifestyle. Nor will it make sure that my sister Jahliya continues to get to live like a Queen. If Phoenix wanna play games wit' me, I'ma buss his brain. That's how that's going to go."

"Shid, I don't care about none of that. All I care about is that five gees and getting back to Milwaukee. I say we go over here and holler at these niggas like ASAP, so I can get my paper. We leaving Memphis tomorrow anyway, so fuck what happens tonight."

"Aiight, that's cool. I need y'all to give me a few minutes to wake up. I'll meet y'all downstairs in like twenty. Bet."

"Bet, lil' cuz. I'm finna catch me a snack anyway." Ja-Michael held his assault rifle up against his shoulder and walked out of the room in his Army fatigues.

Makaroni stood up and stretched his arms over his head. "Damn." He yawned again. "Ain't no way I could live down here. It's always some bullshit popping off."

Montana stepped into the room. "Boy, the last time I checked in here, you were snoring. What the hell are you doing up right now?" She asked hugging him.

He wrapped his arms around her body and squeezed her booty. She wore a short night gown that did very little to shield her lowers. "Stevo and JaMichael just woke me. We gotta ride out to Orange Mound so we can handle some business with a crew called the Duffel Bag Cartel. You ever heard of them?" He asked.

She nodded. "Yeah. That's a crew headed by Phoenix Stevens. He's our distant cousin, but him and JaMichael don't really see eye to eye because of Jahliya."

"Because of Jahliya? What she got to do wit' it?"

"That fool JaMichael is very overprotective of her like you are about me. Phoenix is some type of way. He be at Jahliya like she the finest Queen on earth. I mean, I'm not saying that

she ain't, but he just overdo it. Second to that, Phoenix had a right-hand man called Mikey. Jahliya was rumored to have hit his ass for a few bricks back in the day. Because Jahliya was Phoenix's blood, he rolled with Jahliya over Mikey. They went to war. Mikey moved out to White Haven; the locals call it Black Haven. When he moved out to Black Haven, he mounted up a bunch of troops and they rode beside him and went to war with Phoenix and his Duffel Bag Cartel crew over in Orange Mound. They had that gunplay, and Mikey wound up on the losing end of that battle. Long story short, Orange Mound and Black Haven been warring ever since. When they war though, JaMichael make money. He supplying both sides because don't nobody else wanna deal with the dealers down there that are stuck in the middle of a warzone."

Makaroni rubbed his chin hairs. "Dat's why that nigga had us do what we did. Okay. Now it make sense. Who supposed to be calling shots for Black Haven?"

"Some young dude named Smoke. He used to be down with the Duffel Bag Cartel until he crossed Phoenix." She sighed. "Yeah, Memphis is crazy. That's why we gotta get the fuck out of here."

Makaroni was frozen in place. He felt like he was being used. He didn't understand what JaMichael had up his sleeve, but he knew it had to be something that benefitted him.

"That ain't the reason why I came in here a few times to see if you were woke though. It's mama. I think something ain't right with her because she ain't responded to none of my Facebook messages. That ain't like her. She usually gets back to me right away." Montana felt uneasy.

"Man, you know how mama is when it comes to that social media shit. Sometimes she wit' it, and other times she ain't. She's cooky like that."

"N'all, Mack. I feel it in my soul. Something ain't right. She ain't answering her phone either."

Stevo knocked on the door. "Fuck taking you so long, Makaroni? We gotta holler at these niggas so we can get on back. Time is money, bruh."

"Yeah, aiight, Stevo. Here I come!" Makaroni hollered.

Montana stepped into his face. "What should we do, big bruh? I'm worried about her."

He hugged her to his body. "Call Cassidy. Call Seth. See if they heard from her. Keep hitting her up on social media too. After I handle this business tonight, we gon' bounce out of Memphis tomorrow and go back home to make sure she straight. Besides, we got some work to put in there anyway. Your brother about to come up major, lil' sis. Mark those words."

"I believe you. Just be careful tonight. Can you do that for me?" She wrapped her arm around his neck and looked into his eyes.

"I got you. You already know I do."

She stepped forward and kissed him ever so tenderly. Their lip smacking was loud in the room. She breathed heavily. She felt like she was melting in his arms.

Makaroni backed up. His dick was hard. It hurt. "Aiight, sis, go handle that business. I'll see you in a few hours."

She nodded. "Be safe. Please, Mack."

***

JaMichael pulled the black Excursion into the lot of the Orange Mound apartments. He parked the big truck directly in the center of the complex parking lot. Threw it in park, and loaded his hand pistols into his holsters. "I'm letting you niggas know right now that if Phoenix get to talking out the side of his neck, I'm slumping his bitch ass right then and there. I

need for y'all to have my back. You can't trust these Duffel Bag Cartel niggas. They shysty."

Makaroni pulled his shirt down over his Teflon vest. He had a .45 in the small of his back, and a Glock in his waistband. He was ready for action. "Look, before you get to shooting and all of that, you need to give us a signal. That way we don't get caught off guard."

"Yeah, we don't know how these niggas get down out here, but you do. So, if you feeling like you about to get on that killa shit, you need to smack the table. Wink ya' eye a something." Stevo added.

"Aiight. If I stand up and say you mafuckas don't think fat meat greasy, that a be y'all cue to let them shots rang out with no remorse. Y'all got that?"

"Yeah." Makaroni cocked his Glock.

"Bet those." Stevo felt his adrenalin pumping.

"Aiight, I'ma go and let this nigga know that I'm here. Y'all chill for a minute. I'ma wave y'all over when it's good." He jumped out of the truck and jogged up to the building. They watched him go inside of it after knocking for a few seconds.

"Say, Stevo, I been meaning to ask you somethin' since we left Milwaukee. It's completely random but I still want you to answer the question. Awright."

"Yeah, nigga, what's up?" Stevo kept looking out of the windshield to see when JaMichael would come back to give them the signal.

"Dawg, I always wanted to know what your mother did to you to make you feel the way that you do toward her. Like, why do you hate her so much?"

Stevo was taken completely off guard. "Nigga, we out here ready to go to war with some clowns that we don't even

know. We far away from home. You telling me that's what's on your brain?" He felt himself becoming heated.

"Dawg, I just wanna know. I been wanting to ask you that my whole life. I just never got up the nerve to ask it."

Stevo was hoping that JaMichael came out so he wouldn't have to dive into his personal life, but he didn't see him. "Dawg, what's it to you?"

"I just wanna know, bruh. You my Day One. You know everything about me. That's just a little bit of information that I don't know about you."

"Yeah, well, maybe you don't need to know. You ever thought about that shit? Huh? Have you?"

Makaroni kept his silence. He loved his right hand. He could tell that there was something going on with Stevo underneath the surface. He wanted to find out before they got back to Milwaukee.

"Dawg, my mother sold my sister away to a white family in West Allis." Stevo blurted.

"What?" That was a response that Makaroni wasn't expecting.

"Yeah, she was pregnant with her when we first got up here from Chicago. She wasn't pregnant by my father either. She was pregnant by her high school boyfriend. Some nigga named Neyo. When we got up here to Milwaukee, shit was real hard for us. She could barely afford to feed me. We were living from house to house. She never had enough money to do nothing. Well, two months before she had my sister, one of the landlords offered her a hundred thousand dollars for the female child in her stomach. She didn't flinch. My father didn't want her to have the baby anyway because he knew it wasn't his. Plus, he was fuckin' wit' them drugs real tough back then anyway. But yeah, she sold my sister. The same dude she sold my sister to wound up getting locked up for a

bunch of rapes and shit down the road. I can only imagine what he did to her. Even though I never met my sister, I love her. I love her to this day, and I hate my mother because of what she did. I hate Seth bitch ass too. That punk ain't no father of mine." He clenched his jaw. "I'll never forgive her, Makaroni. Never. I'ma find my sister too. One of these days I really am."

"Do you even know her name?" Makaroni felt horrible for his homie. He got to imagining what life would've been like if he would've never known Montana. The feeling was enough to make him sick.

"Jada. That's all I know. I don't know her last name or nothing, but Cassidy do."

Makaroni nodded. He rested his hand on Stevo's shoulder. "I appreciate you going there with me, dawg. If you ever wanna find her, I'm wit' you."

"Appreciate that, homie. Soon I am. We gotta get our money right first. Then I'm going to find my lil' sister. That's my word."

"Cool." Makaroni rubber-necked to scan the area. "Man, JaMichael sho' taking a long ass time." His phone vibrated. He took it off of his hip. There was a text from Montana: *Mack, we gotta get back home. They just found mama. She messed up real bad. Life threatening injuries. Call me. ASAP.* Makaroni's stomach dropped.

"Fuck wrong wit' you?" Stevo asked.

Before he could answer the question, two black vans pulled up in back of the Excursion, boxing it in. Ten men jumped out with masks on their faces, and guns in their hands. They surrounded their truck. Phoenix ran around to the front of the Excursion and aimed an assault rifle at the windshield. His red beam lasered into the darkness, searching for a target. "Y'all got three seconds to come up out of that truck or we

finna blow this bitch up. This is yo final warning!" He hollered.

Stevo ducked lower into his seat as the beam came searching for a target inside of their truck. He gazed into the rearview mirror and saw the black Excursion on their bumper. It would be impossible for either him or Makaroni to jump behind Ja-Michael's steering wheel to make a retreat. "Dis shit don't seem right, Makaroni. It's something real fishy about this." He snapped.

Makaroni was trying his best to remain calm. Four men jumped out of the Excursion with assault rifles in their hands, and beams on top of their weapons, aiming their guns at the window of the truck. He cocked his pistol, fearing the worst. It had only been less than a week since he and Stevo went on a rampage right there in Orange Mound. They left multiple bodies lying in the streets per JaMichael's request. Now they were targets.

"Bruh, I don't give a fuck how many niggas it is right now. I ain't finna go out like no punk. They finna have to bury me." Stevo hissed.

"You already know that. Fuck you wanna do? Whatever you 'bout, nigga, I'm 'bout." Makaroni was locked and loaded. He felt deep within his heart that they were about to die. He felt like JaMichael dropped the ball and allowed for them to be caught slipping and stuck in an impossible situation to get out of. In that moment he hated his cousin.

Phoenix raised the assault rifle higher. "Oh, so ma'fuckas really think I'm playin'? Aiight den." He took a few steps back. "Chop this bitch down."

Boom. Boom. Boom. Boom.

His crew let off slug after slug. Their bullets ripped into the body of the truck, rocking it from side to side. Bright sparks from the slugs hitting the metal, illuminating the

16

parking lot. The windows burst. The Duffel Bag Cartel kept shooting. The trucks tires whistled and went flat. Phoenix smiled. His Choppah vibrated in his arms. He didn't give a fuck if he killed both men. He knew that the truck belonged to his cousin JaMichael but he didn't care. As far as he was concerned, JaMichael had his men on *his* turf. In Memphis, that act was punishable by death. He spat five more rounds.

Makaroni fell to the floor of the truck, covering his head as glass busted onto his back. He could hear the bullets slamming into exteriors of the truck. He was praying that they didn't cut through and hit either himself or Stevo. He felt betrayed. He wondered why JaMichael would lead him into the Orange Mound where he would be put to death. It didn't make sense. They were supposed to make so much money together. All three of them. On top of that they were family.

Stevo clenched his jaw so hard he could taste blood on his tongue. If the group of hittas didn't kill him, he was vowing revenge. He felt like a pussy. He was laid on his stomach with his head covered just like Makaroni. He felt that this wasn't a position for any real killa to be in. He felt emasculated.

Phoenix held up his hand. "Aiight. Hold up." He ordered. The shooting ceased. He walked closer to the truck. He eyed it closely. "Say, Mane, if you ma'fuckas still alive, y'all better say something, or dis here grenade finna be tossed into that there windshield." He promised.

He wasn't worried about the police responding to the shots. He knew that the Orange Mound had been red-listed by the government. That meant that law enforcement would respond as slowly as they wanted to. Often times they didn't come at all. They expected and hoped that the current occupants of Orange Mound would kill themselves before they were all kicked out of their habitat and force to find other areas to populate. The city was looking to turn Orange Mound into

a bunch of condominiums and renting them out to the upper crust of Memphis.

"Yo, Mack, what the fuck we do?" Stevo asked.

"Man, fuck that nigga. If he gon' blow us up, then he gon' have to come on wit' it. I think if we expose ourselves they gon' wind up killing us anyway." He whispered.

"I ain't finna go out like no bitch, Mack. Fuck this. They finna have to kill me like a soldier." He rolled onto his back and got ready to sit up. It made him feel sick to the stomach that this night was his death date. But he quickly made peace with it.

"Fuck it, bruh. You already know I'm riding wit' you. I love you, dawg." Makaroni took a deep breath and hopped up.

Stevo came to his knees and peered out of the window. He saw three dudes standing, looking over to Phoenix as if they were looking for him to give them their next order. He took the upper hand and used it. He aimed and fired kill shots. All facials. *Bocka. Bocka. Bocka. Bocka.*

Makaroni aimed directly at Phoenix, and finger fucked his gun. *Boo-wah! Boo-wah! Boo-wah! Boo-wah!*

Phoenix felt the slugs punch into his vest, knocking him off of his feet. It felt like his chest had been doused with gasoline and set on fire. He scooted backward on the grass and held the trigger to his assault rifle, chopping at the truck.

Stevo slid out of the windshield of the truck. He jumped to the concrete and took off running behind one of the Duffel Bag Cartel members that dropped his gun after seeing his homies' heads explode beside him. He ran as fast as he could. When he got to the apartment doors, he tried to open it, but found it locked. Stevo rushed him. He swung his gun and slammed it into the side of his head.

"Aw fuck!" The dude turned around and tried to bull-rush him, but Stevo was too quick. He fired and knocked the left

side of his face into the grass. The dude kept on shaking. He hollered as loud as he could. It sounded like he was groaning through a funnel.

Makaroni had a hard time getting through the back window of the truck. By the time he was on solid ground Phoenix had gotten up and made a run for it into the buildings. This infuriated Makaroni. He smelled his blood. He wanted his life. He refused to leave Memphis until he had hit. He didn't give a fuck if they shared the same bloodline.

Stevo jogged over to him with his guns smoking. "Nigga, you good?" he asked. His throat was scratchy. He was hoping his asthma didn't act up. He'd left his pump at Jahliya's mansion.

Makaroni nodded. "I don't know what the fuck they thought this was."

"Me either, but shit ain't sweet. I hate these Memphis niggas!" Stevo snapped. "Where the fuck is JaMichael?"

As if on cue JaMichael came staggering out of the gangway of the apartment complex four apartments up from where they stood. He held his hand over a bullet wound on his shoulder and stomach.

Makaroni took off running toward him. Just before he got to his side, JaMichael fell to his knees and fainted. Makaroni fell beside him. "What the fuck happened, cuz? Aw shit."

Stevo jogged up and aimed his gun down at JaMichael's face. "Seem to me he already on his way out. Might as well finish his punk ass."

"No!" Makaroni covered him with his body. "Nigga, calm yo trigger-happy ass down. Clearly, he was blindsided. We gotta get him the fuck outta here." Makaroni hit up Jahliya.

Stevo felt nothing for JaMichael. He wanted to stank him. He wanted to send him on his way with no remorse. In his

heart, he felt that JaMichael was dirty. He couldn't be trusted. Taking his life would have been a cake walk to him.

Makaroni looked up to him. "Dawg, she on her way. I don't know what the fuck is going on but something ain't right. We gotta get back to Milwaukee too. Montana say they found my mother and she fucked up. It's all bad."

Stevo heard that news and snapped out of his murderous zone. "What? Aw shit, Mack. What the fuck is going on?"

All Makaroni could do was lower his head. "I don't know. But we gotta get back home and find out."

Stevo nodded. "Ma'fuckas in trouble, dawg. My heart can't get no colder."

"Mine can, and it is." Makaroni said, holding a bleeding JaMichael against himself.

Chapter 2

Two days later, Makaroni and Stevo rolled into Milwaukee with a lot on their minds. It was a snowy day. The traffic coming into the city was slow. There were big plows that operated on the highways to clear up as much of the snow as they possibly could. When they finally got to the Greyhound bus station, the weather had gotten worst. The snow dropped from the sky steadily. It made it hard for a person to see in front of them.

Stevo stepped off the big bus and zipped up his Bomber jacket. He squinted to avoid the snow from flying into them. "Man, it's colder than a bitch. I don't miss this shit."

Makaroni felt sick as soon as his boots hit the snow. He couldn't help but to worry about Maisey, his mother. She had been very vague with the details that she'd given him over the phone. Her only words were that she was better, and that they can never steal her joy. Makaroni took that to mean that the worst possible thing had happened, but it hadn't been enough to break her. "Man, since we downtown already we might as well swing a couple blocks over and visit my mother. She right over at Sinai Samaritan."

Stevo nodded as the wind blew harder. He grabbed his luggage from under the bus. "Aiight, that sound like a plan. Grab yo bags, bruh. You already know what's in these ma'fuckas." He spoke about the eight kilos of the Rebirth that Jahliya had given them per JaMichael's orders. Each brick could be bussed down four times, and it would've still been the strongest dope in Milwaukee.

Makaroni grabbed his things and sighed. "Come on, dawg, we can walk this lil' short distance."

Ghost

"Hell n'all! Nigga, that's like ten blocks away. It's too cold to be doing all of that. We need to either catch a cab or jump on the Twelve Street bus. It go right past the hospital."

"Aiight, well, you do what you gotta do. I'm finna trek on over there." Makaroni walked off with his head down. He didn't feel like arguing with Stevo. He had way too much on his mind. He was worried about how the sight of his mother was going to affect him. More importantly than that, he tried to piece together who could have had enough gall to attack her in the first place. Most of the people in their neighborhood knew that Maisey had a lunatic for a son. Messing with her was nothing short of a death sentence.

Stevo allowed for him to get a short distance away before he caught up to him. "Damn, yousa stubborn ass nigga. You know I ain't finna let you walk by yourself."

Makaroni shrugged. "I'm fucked up mentally, Stevo. I'm scared what this shit finna look like."

"Man, all we can do is find out everything that she know. The more she tell us, the better. We'll be able to piece together the puzzle. As soon as we do, you already know it's curtains for whoever hurt her."

"Yeah. You muthafuckin' right it is." The wind blew harshly. Ice like snowflakes crashed into Makaroni's face. His cheeks were frozen. He sniffed snot back into his brownish red nose, putting a pep in his step so they could reach the hospital quicker.

***

Thirty minutes later, Maisey sat up in her hospital bed feeling a bit lightheaded from the morphine they were pumping into her system. She situated herself on the bed and closed her eyelids tightly. She prayed for the dizzy spell to go away.

Dizziness always led to nausea for her. There was nothing worst to her than throwing up.

The nurse, a short, white and skinny woman, knocked on Maisey's hospital door, and stuck her head inside. "Hey there, Ms. Stevens. I have a few visitors here that want to see you."

Maisey kept her eyes closed. She was sure it was the police coming back to bug her. She didn't feel like dealing with them. She also had no intentions of helping them find Stacy and his crew. She didn't believe in the criminal justice system. She believed in street justice. An eye for an eye. "Tell whoever it is that I'm not feeling well. I don't want to talk or visit right now. Tell them to go away."

The nurse smiled warmly. "I'll do just that." She pulled her head out of the door. She stepped away from Maisey's room and headed down the hallway. She walked right up to a waiting Makaroni. "Um, you're going to have to try to get into contact with her later. She is refusing all visitors right now. She says that she isn't feeling well."

"What? Bitch, you tripping." Makaroni snapped. "I'm her son. She gon' wanna see me. He pointed at his chest. "Did you tell her that I'm here?" he asked.

She nodded, backing away. "I sure did." She lied.

"Well, fuck what you talking about. That's my mama. I'm finna go and see what's good with her. I don't care what you talking about."

"Sir, if you do, I'll be forced to call security."

"The police? Really, bitch?" Stevo added, jumping into the verbal disagreement.

"That's right." The nurse slowly backed away from them, headed toward the nursing station.

***

The elevator dinged before the doors opened. Cassidy stepped off with flowers in her hand. She didn't care to speak with the hospital staff. She knew exactly where Maisey's room was. She headed there. She stepped inside of it and placed the flowers that she'd brought into an empty vase next to her bed. Then she leaned over and kissed Maisey on the cheek. "Good morning, sunshine."

Maisey opened her eyes with a smile on her face after hearing the familiar voice. "Hey, girl." Her voice was dry and scratchy. She coughed and beat on her chest.

"Girl, they ain't got no juice for you?" Cassidy asked looking around and spotting none. "Don't worry, I'll be right back."

"Girl, don't worry about it." Maisey called still feeling dizzy.

Cassidy waved her off. She stepped into the hallway to see if she could spot a nurse. The left side of the hallway where the elevators were was clear of nurses. She looked to her right and had to squint to make sure that she wasn't seeing things. Then she was sure that she saw both Makaroni and Stevo. They looked to be arguing with a security guard. Cassidy took off running down the hallway. She wanted to diffuse the situation quickly. She knew that both Stevo and Makaroni had terrible tempers. She couldn't stand to see them get into trouble. When she got to them, she was forced to pull Stevo backward. His fist was balled tight. He was seconds away from knocking the hospital security staff out. "Baby, what's the matter?" She asked him.

He yanked away from her. At first, he didn't know who she was. After seeing that it was his mother, he softened just a tad. "Cassidy, they trying to stop us from seeing Maisey. They talking about she don't want to see us."

"What? That's not true." She mugged the nurse. "She been worried sick for the both of you. Who told you this?"

Makaroni pointed to the skinny nurse. "Shorty goofy ass right there."

The nurse blushed. "Well, it's what she told me."

The guard, a heavyset, balding white man, that was seconds away from contacting the local police department looked down at the nurse. "Ma'am, do you want these hoodlums removed or not?"

"Hoodlums?" Cassidy jerked her head back, taken off guard by that comment. "Excuse me, officer whatever yo name is, but these are my young men. They are not hoodlums. This young man here is very concerned about his mother who is down there laying in her hospital bed. She wants to see him."

The officer ignored Cassidy. He didn't like her skin complexion, nor did he like the colors of Makaroni and Stevo. If it was up to him, he would've had all three of them thrown out of the hospital. He cleared his throat at the nurse again. "Ma'am do you want me to get rid of them?"

The nurse hung her head. "No, it wouldn't be necessary. I'll simply check with Ms. Stevens to see if she would like for them to visit with her. If she says yes, then they can. If it's a no, then they have to leave the premises at once. Okay?" She looked them all over.

Makaroni was fuming. "Tell my mother that her son Makaroni is here. That's all you gotta do."

The nurse nodded. "I'm going to do that right now." She headed down the hallway to Maisey's hospital room.

***

Makaroni situated himself more comfortably on Maisey's bed. He held her against his chest. His strong arms wrapped

around her body. "Aiight, Ma, now tell me who did this stuff to you." It had been the first time he'd seen his mother with a black eye. Her face was a bit swollen, and she looked as if she were in pain. It broke his heart. He kept on swallowing his spit to keep from shedding a tear. His mother was his world.

"I don't know who the boys were, Derez, but they know you and Stevo."

Stevo paced, seething. He couldn't believe that somebody had gotten a hold of Maisey. She had always been such a sweet woman to him. He actually loved her more than he did his own mother. He couldn't wait to find out who hurt her. He promised to take their life with no mercy.

"Awright, mama. Did you hear any names? Can you describe what any of them looked like? Or did they have a mask on the whole time?" Makaroni asked holding her tighter.

"They wore masks at first. Then they took them off. I can barely remember the other two faces, but the one that raped me over and over, I can remember his face clear as day."

Makaroni eased from the bed. "Wait a minute. You mean to tell me that one of these niggas did that to you?" Tears seeped out of his eyes. He was so angry that he was shaking.

Maisey nodded. "Yeah, baby. Repeatedly."

"All of them, or just one of them?" Stevo asked. He couldn't even look her in the eye. He felt bad for her. He already knew that he and Makaroni were about to go on a killing spree until they fully annihilated the person that had done Maisey in.

"Just him." She whispered.

Makaroni fell to his knees beside the bed. He could no longer hold his weight up. He felt weak. "Mama, please tell me what he looked like. Please. I need to find this nigga or I ain't never gon' be able to sleep again." He was dead serious.

Maisey understood how much her son loved her. She really didn't want to get him into any trouble, but she knew that Stacy had to pay for his sins. There was no other way. "He was dark skinned. A little taller than me. He had short dread locks. There were tattoos all over his face."

Makaroni jumped up. "You talkin' about Stacy bitch ass." His fists were balled so tight that his fingers were steady cracking.

"That's his name. I remember one of those lil' boys slipping up and calling him that. He hit the boy in the mouth as soon as he had."

Stevo's jaw dropped. Stacy had struck again. First, he'd burned down Stevo's parents' house, and now he'd forced himself onto Maisey. That meant war. "Bruh, you already know that it's whatever you wanna do. I'm 'bout whatever you 'bout. All you gotta do is say what's really good."

Makaroni wiped the tears from his eyes. "Mama, are you okay? That's all I gotta know."

She blinked tears. "Cassidy. Stevo. Give me us a second. Let me talk to my baby in private."

Stevo nodded in understanding. He walked over and kissed her on the forehead. "Be strong, Maisey. We gon' handle that nigga for you. I promise you that."

She smiled. "Stevo, you chill for a minute. Don't do nothing crazy. Okay?" She placed her open palm on the side of his face.

He took her hand and kissed the back of it. "I can't promise you that. Dawg, I'll meet you downstairs." With that, he laid her hand back on to her stomach and left the room.

Cassidy kissed Maisey on the cheek. "When y'all done talking, I'll be back up here. I love you, girl."

"I love you too." Maisey returned.

Ghost

Makaroni waited until they were out of the room before his tears dropped. "Mama, I'm letting you know right now that I'm finna kill that nigga so cold that he gon' regret ever puttin' his hands on you. Don't nobody touch you and get away with it. Nobody." He snapped. He saw that she was about to say something, and he interrupted her. "Don't try to stop me either. That bitch ass nigga gotta go."

Maisey shook her head. "I would never try to stop you from defending me. I am your mother. That is your place." She scooted up the bed on her elbows. After she was as comfortable as she could be, she took a sip from the juice that Cassidy bought her and laid back. "I ain't never killed nobody in my life, Makaroni. I always tried my best to live on the right side of the street. I go to church. I read my Bible. I love the Lord. I don't know how much more our Maker can ask from me." She adjusted herself on the bed again. The machines in her room continued to beep every so often. "Baby, when you find him, I wanna be the one to take his life. I want to make him pay for what he did to me. Do you understand this?"

Makaroni was shocked at what she was getting at. He couldn't imagine his mother hurting anybody. "Ma, I don't think I'ma be able to control myself when I find him. This nigga done been inside of you. He defiled you." He punched his fist and imagined the last time he'd seen Stacy's mother. She worked at the Public Aid office right on 12th and Vliet Street. He imagined doing to Stacy's mother what Stacy had done to his, and the image made him shake.

"Makaroni, come here, son."

Makaroni walked over to her until he was standing in her face. "What's up, mama?"

She wiped away his tears with her thumbs. "Baby, I know that you are broken up because of what he did to me. But I

need for you to keep your head in the Game. You have a lot riding on what you brought back from Memphis."

Makaroni was taken off guard. "What are you talking about?"

She rubbed his face. "Your cousin Jahliya told me what's up. We have a stronger relationship than you and Montana realize, but I digress. You need to focus on getting our family financially secure in the Game. Now that you are involved with Rubio Flores there is no room for error. You'll catch Stacy. When you do, you bring him to mama, alive. Promise me that." She held his face and looked into his eyes. "Can you do that?"

Makaroni nodded. "I'll do anything for you, Queen. I got you."

Ghost

Chapter 3

A week later, Stevo opened shop inside of a small duplex on 34th and Vliet right across from a school. He knew that the chances of him getting knocked were higher because he was slanging in a school zone, but he didn't care. The landlord was a heroin addict from West Allis. He was looking to get rid of the property for a few ounces of the Rebirth after testing the product. Stevo couldn't help but to seize the come up.

Paul sat crossed-leg on the floor with the syringe stuck deep in his arm. He pushed down on the feeder and injected the poison into his system. His eyes rolled into the back of his head. Adrenalin mixed with euphoria rushed all over his body. He felt like he was climaxing and was on fire at the same time. He couldn't help smiling. He laid straight out on his back, naked.

Dope Fiend Sheryl crawled over to him and pulled the syringe out of his arm. She placed it beside him. Sheryl was a dark shade of Black. Skinny with brown eyes. "Baby, we might as well do his deal so we have a whole lot of this shit. Ain't no telling when it's gone run out." She said kissing all over Paul's chest.

Stevo walked over and knelt beside him. He held the pen in one hand, and the deed to the duplex in the other. "Sign dis ma'fucka so we can get a move on. Y'all holding up my operation." He growled.

Sheryl grabbed the two items and handed them to Paul. "Huh,, baby. Sign it. You got plenty other properties. Sign it and let's get the fuck up out of here." She helped him to come to a seated position.

Paul sat up and signed the document. "Here you go, Stevo. It's yours. Just always do me right."

Stevo grabbed his finger and tapped it inside of the ink. Then he pressed it to the document and stepped away from them. "Y'all got ten minutes to get out of my shit." He dropped the dope on Paul's chest.

Makaroni shook his head while seated at the table. "Bruh, you a fool. You said you was finna find us a crib to pop out of, and you definitely did that."

"You muthafuckin' right I did. Tonight, we finna have this user's party. Ma'fuckas gotta pay fifty dollars to get in. Once they in here, we gon' pump them up with a quarter brick of The Rebirth. Get they ass hooked. Then it's curtains. Word won't take long to spread in this area, especially since it's been a bunch of twenty percent Boy floating through the city. Yo, Sheryl, you sure we gon' have one hell of a turn out tonight?" Stevo asked.

Sheryl helped Paul into his pants. "Daddy-O, you just leave all of that to me. I been networking. This house about to be so full that you ain't gon' know what to do. Trust me on that." She said, sounding optimistic.

Stevo smiled. "Bitch, it better. I got a lot riding on yo word. You fail me, and I'm done fuckin' wit' you."

Sheryl poked out her juicy bottom lip. "Baby, you ain't gon' have to worry about that. I'ma definitely do my part. You'll see. Come on, Paul." She helped him out the back door and to his Volvo that was parked behind the house.

Makaroni finished bagging up five thousand dime bags of The Rebirth. He dropped the last bag into a Ziploc and scooted away from the table. "I'm ready to get this money, Stevo. Straight up. Christmas is right around the corner."

Stevo received a text from Keaira. *I need some money. I'm broke. Steven need diapers. What's up?* She ended with a bunch of angry faced emojis. Stevo sighed. His baby mother was always getting on his last nerve. It seemed like it was

always something with her. "I agree, dawg. That's why as soon as we have this dope party our chips should shoot through the roof. This Rebirth ain't no ma'fuckin' punk. It already got us a crib. This only the beginning, though." He put his phone away.

Makaroni yawned and stretched his hands over his head. "Aiight, so how we finna do this?"

Stevo watched Sheryl lead Paul out of the door.

He was high as a kite. With every step he took he would laugh, and hug closer to her body. "I ain't never felt this good before, Sheryl. You got the rest of my dope? Huh?" He asked looking up at her.

Sheryl nodded. "I got you, baby. Don't I always? You don't worry about nothin'." She assured him. She winked at Stevo. "I'll be back tonight with my crew. Not no broke ass users either. Trust aunty, I got this." She closed the door behind her.

Stevo stood there for a minute. "Aiight, so she finna group up a bunch of users. They gon' come and test us out. After they see that we got the real deal, we gon' load our phones up with their information and go from there. I give it a few months and we should be able to make our rounds through the city. Lock this ma'fucka down."

Makaroni rubbed his chin as he listened on in agreement. He still felt some type of way about Stacy and what he'd done to Maisey, but in the moment it was essential that he paid attention to what Stevo was saying. Makaroni was a stick-up kid at heart. He knew how to hustle, but hustling wasn't his first love. Now that he and Stevo were knee-deep in the water with Rubio Flores, the deadly Cartel leader, Makaroni felt that it was in his best interest to master the dope game. If he didn't, it could cost him his life.

"But, anyway, bruh this shit should be simple as two plus two. The Rebirth gon' sell itself. All we gotta do is set up the best networking strategy to assist The Rebirth and we should be good." He rested his hand on Makaroni's shoulder. "And, Mack, even though we finna get it in on this hustlin' shit, that don't mean that Stacy finna get a pass. We still at his neck like a tie and a suit. You feel me?"

"Yeah, dawg. I need to hurry up and get to rocking this dog food so I can take my mind off of that nigga. Stevo, every time I close my eyes all I see is his face. I can't believe that we ain't ran into him yet. What are the odds?"

Stevo shrugged. "Milwaukee small. I wouldn't worry about it. Sooner or later we gon' run into him, and when we do, it's curtains." He frowned. "That chump gon' pay for what he did. You better believe that. But for now, let's focus in on the hustle. Cool?"

Makaroni held his head down. "Yeah, cool."

***

That night, Sheryl was beating on the door to the Trap house at eleven o'clock sharp. Makaroni opened the door with a .40 Glock tucked into the small of his back. The wind rushed into the Trap, followed by a bit of snow. It was coming down like crazy outside. Sheryl stood before him dressed in an all-white snow suit. She looked like a run down child. He looked past her shoulder and saw that there was a bunch of cars parking in the front of the Trap. As soon as the cars parked, they made their way up behind Sheryl.

"I told you I wouldn't fail y'all. I'm bringing the whole city out that get down like me. You boys are about to make some serious dough." She winked at him.

"Yeah, well, I don't give a fuck how many people pulling up. As long as they hit my hand with fifty dollars before they come through this threshold."

"Aw, baby, that was already established. If they ain't got your money, then you can turn they ass right around. Speaking of which." She unzipped her snow suit and went into her blouse. Once there she pulled a fifty dollar bill out of her bra. "Here you go. May I pass?" She licked her juicy lips.

"Yeah, gone 'head. You good to go."

She stepped past Makaroni smelling like cooking grease, and unwashed scalp. "Stevo? Stevo, baby, where are you at?" She called disappearing into the Trap.

Makaroni stood at the door collecting his funds as each addict stepped up to him. After he checked the fifty to make sure that it was real, he allowed for them to pass by him. He stood at the door for thirty minutes, until the Trap was so full that it looked like they were throwing a house party.

Stevo stepped up to him. "Say, bruh, that's it. Can't nobody else come into this ma'fucka. Ain't no more room." He tapped him on the shoulder so he could see how they were packed from wall to wall. Stevo had put on an Isley Brothers album. Slow music crooned out of the speakers. The scent of the house was starting to smell bad already. It was making his stomach turn.

Makaroni locked the door and closed the curtains. He made his way through the crowd behind Stevo. When they got into the living room, he took a seat at the tables and plopped a pillowcase on top of it. Inside of the pillowcase were a thousand hits of the Rebirth. Nice dosages that were sure to hook the new customers. "Aiight, you ma'fuckas form an orderly line. One hit at a time. We gon' do this shit the right way." He announced.

Stevo waited until they lined up. Then he walked up and down the line making sure that it was in order. "Single file. When you get yo work, go into the front room and sit on the floor. This that new shit. Be thankful that you are the very first in the city to get a load of it. And as strong as it is today, is the same potency that it will have tomorrow. You got our words on that."

Makaroni served one fiend at a time. It took him a half hour to serve each one. When he was done, he stood up and watched all around the room as they injected themselves with the Rebirth.

Stevo could smell money. He looked on as one after another of the fiends moaned out loud as the Rebirth was shot into their system. They would close their eyes with a big smile on their face. Others frowned. Others shivered and scooted closer with their backs to the wall. They placed their heads in their laps, nodding in and out. Every so often they would come to and start to scratch themselves.

Makaroni watched this go on for a full twenty minutes. He took a seat back at the table. "Aiight, now everybody get back in line for your next dosage. This time I need your contact information, and Stevo here is going to give you ours. If you are interested in shopping with us from here on out, use these numbers. But if you fuck with us, then it's just us. If we find out that you are shopping with anybody else, then we're through fuckin wit' you. There is also a reward for those that can bring us footage of anybody else in this room shopping with another dope boy outside of us. We'll reward you on the spot. This shit is serious. Loyalty has to be established immediately. Y'all got that?" He asked.

They nodded all around the room in agreement while they scratched themselves. The funk in the room was getting

horrible. The fiends lined up as if they were waiting to get on a ride at Great America.

Stevo walked up and down the line suspiciously. If anything or anybody looked out of order he was ready to put them out. "Y'all do us right, and we'll treat you good. We ain't looking to get over on nobody. We'll always make sure we got the best work in town."

"Yeah." Makaroni continued to serve each hype again. Once all of them were taken care of they went back to their places where they shot up the Rebirth. He couldn't take his mind off of Maisey. He wondered if she was okay now that she was back home. He prayed that Cassidy was looking after her. He couldn't wait to get home so he could check on her himself. He missed her.

Stevo couldn't believe the turn out. He counted a hundred addicts. He knew there would've been more if he hadn't told Makaroni to lock the door, and stop them from coming in. He felt proud. He felt giddy. He imagined the money that was sure to come, and it made him overly excited. He was tired of being a bum. The Rebirth was sure to change their status in the world. He was sure of that.

They stayed up serving the fiends until the wee hours of the night. When they ran through an entire quarter bird, they shut down shop and sent all of the fiends home. When it was all said and done, they were fifteen thousand dollars richer off of the party and sales. They split the money down the middle, each taking home seventy-five hundred a piece. For both men it was a come up, and only the beginning.

Chapter 4

It had been two weeks since Makaroni and Stevo had been back from visiting the South. The snow had taken a break from being a burden to the city of Milwaukee. Cassidy peeked out of the window to see if Makaroni had pulled up to the front of the house. When she saw that the parking space was empty, she became irritated.

Seth stepped into the living room and snuck behind her. He slid his arms around her waist and planted a kiss on the back of her neck. "Hey, Foxy."

Cassidy jumped from the sudden contact. When she discovered that it was none other than her husband she eased out of his embrace. "Boy, stop. I don't feel like playing right now." She moved him out of the way to see if Makaroni had turned on to the block yet. She searched up and down both sides of the street. There was still no sign of him.

Seth stood there for a second. He was six feet tall, light skinned with brown eyes. He kept a short haircut. His waves were all natural. "Cassidy, what's the matter with you?" He asked, disgruntled.

She rolled her eyes, still peering out of the window. "Seth, I don't feel like arguing with you right now. Ain't you supposed to be getting to work? Ain't you gon' be late?"

Seth frowned. "Cassidy, what the fuck is wrong with you? Why have you been acting so funny toward me over the past few weeks?"

Cassidy turned away from the window. She looked him right in the eyes. "Maybe it's because we are still living with somebody else. Or maybe, it's because instead of you figuring out a way to get a roof back over our heads, you choose to work less. You think our insurance company is going to save us out of this rut? Its freaking ridiculous."

"That's what this is all about? You think that I should be doing more, when I am doing the best that I can? Really?" He shook his head. "None of this shit is my fault. None of it. I swear year after year, you get crazier. One of these days, I'ma leave out that door and never come back."

"You been saying that for years, yet here you are." She rolled her eyes and turned back to the window just as Makaroni pulled up to the curb, rolling a rented burgundy Chrysler 300. She felt giddy. She didn't know how she was going to move in on him, but one thing was sure and that's that she was. She'd gone crazy missing him. For her, he was a complete change of pace from Seth. Her walk on the wild side. Her chance at doing something that brought excitement to her life, even though the stakes were high.

"Baby, can we please talk about things? We need to get an understanding before things get too far gone." Seth stepped behind her again. The sight of the yellow mini skirt did something to him. Her bronzed thighs were hefty, sticking out of it. They were well oiled. Her perfume brought back memories of their many passion-filled nights. He was still deep in love with Cassidy. He felt that he always would be.

"Seth, I need space for the moment. We'll talk when you get back home tonight. Okay? I promise." She watched Makaroni step out of the Chrysler and dust his clothes off. He slid his Chanel glasses over his eyes before he slammed the door to his whip.

Seth grabbed her by the wrist and turned her around so that she was facing him. "Cassidy, maybe when I get home tonight, I can take you out to dinner? Maybe we could hit up one of our old spots. We could sit and chat? What do you think?"

Cassidy heard Makaroni's footsteps leading up to the porch. She needed to get Seth out of the house fast. She was growing more and more excited about what she had in mind

with her son's right-hand man. "Okay, baby, that sounds good." She stepped forward and hugged him.

"I love you." Seth moved his head back, and then forward. He began to make out with Cassidy as passionately as he could possibly muster. He felt her trying to resist him, and that only made him try harder. His hands gripped her round ass under the skirt.

Makaroni walked into his mother's duplex and was met with the sight of Seth rubbing all over Cassidy's ass. They kissed hungrily and loudly. He stood transfixed by the sight before him. "Damn, I see y'all trying to keep this marriage alive and strong." He laughed.

Cassidy finally pushed Seth off of her. She wiped her lips with the back of her hand. She felt embarrassed and upset that she had been caught by Makaroni. She mugged Seth. "Not cool, Seth. I said that we would talk about things tonight. And that's what you do to me?"

Seth broke into a fit of laughter. "Girl, shut up. You're my wife. I can kiss yo ass if I want to." He extended his hand to Makaroni and shook up with him. "What's up, son? How you been?"

"Cool." Makaroni returned. He kept his eyes on Cassidy. He could tell that she was upset.

She turned her back to him, unable to look into his eyes. She pulled down her short skirt as far as she could. Her ass poked out like a belly.

Seth eyed her. "Look, I gotta go to work. I'll see you later, Cass. I love you."

She ignored him. She took a seat on the couch and crossed her thick thighs. She was so mad that she felt like screaming. She couldn't believe that Seth would choose to be all over her at such an inconvenient time. They hadn't touched each other in weeks.

Seth shook up with Makaroni again. "See if you can talk some sense into her. Something going on with her, but I can't figure it out. That's my baby though." He looked over to her again. She avoided his eyes. "Yeah, I'm out." He left the house, locking the door behind him.

Makaroni stepped in front of Cassidy. "What? Ma, I don't get no hug or nothin'?"

She looked up at him with her pure brown eyes. She stood up and slid her arms around his body. "I missed you, baby. I been going through hell over here." Her face snuggled into the crux of his neck, smelling his Bulgari cologne.

Makaroni slid his hands under her skirt and rubbed all over her hot flesh, kneading the cheeks of her backside. They felt hot and heavy. "You been missing me, huh? I been missing you too, ma." His fingers pulled her thin strip to the side and slid into her crack. Her sex lips were puffy. Freshly shaven, with dew on them. His middle finger found her hole and sunk deep.

Cassidy closed her eyes and moaned into his neck. "I need you, baby. I feel so low. I'm stressed. I don't know when we're going to be able to move out of here. I just need to forget about my reality for a minute. Can you help mama wit' that?" She moaned.

Makaroni's finger dipped in and out of her slowly. She would grip it with her walls, then back up on it. By the third stroke, it was dripping with her honey. "You gon' give me some of this pussy, ma? Huh?"

She sucked all over his neck. Her hand snuck between them and into his pants. She took a hold of his member and squeezed it. It was hot and growing by the second. Her thumb went back and forth over the head. "I need you, baby. I want some of this young dick right now." She dropped to her knees,

stroking him. She pulled the skin of his dick all the way backward and wet her lips.

"Show me, mama." Makaroni looked down at her with his piece extended.

***

Seth slammed his hands on the steering wheel of the car as it cut off, and sputtered. It rolled for ten yards and came to a slow stop. He threw it in park and cursed under his breath. He sat there for a moment calming himself. Then he turned the key in the ignition. It coughed but didn't start. He turned it back off and pumped his foot on the gas. He tried the ignition again. Nothing happened. "Fuck! Not today!" He hollered. "Now I gotta have her ass give me a ride to work. I don't feel like hearing this girl mouth." He snapped. He shook his head and tried the car again. Still nothing.

Finally, after five more tries he got out and pushed it into a parking space. He glanced at his watch and saw that he was thirty minutes away from being late. He jogged back toward the house. He needed a ride. He was hoping Makaroni wouldn't be opposed to giving him one. He wanted to avoid asking Cassidy. He already felt emasculated enough because it had been a month since they'd been living with Maisey after their house burned to the ground by a fire that had been set by none other than Stacy and his crew. Seth picked up the pace. He couldn't afford to be late. He needed his job.

***

Makaroni opened Cassidy's thighs wide and pushed her knees to her chest so he could see that that pussy bust wide open. Her brown folds looked good to him. He was obsessed with older women. He didn't understand why, but older

women drove him crazy. It was something about their bodies, and their demeanors that made him feel some type of way.

He pressed his nose to Cassidy's pussy and sniffed up and down her slit. His tongue followed the path of her groove. He opened her petals wider, found her clitoris and ran circles around it with his tongue, slurping up her juices.

"Unn! Mack! Shit!" She squeezed her breasts together. Pulled on the nipples that were exposed. Makaroni had pulled her titties over the tops of her bra. The nipples were hard and yearning to be sucked by him. "Eat me, baby. Unn! It feel so good."

Makaroni slipped two fingers into her groove, and finger-fucked her swiftly. He sucked on her clit the entire time.

Cassidy couldn't take it. She took two deep breaths and held them. Then came hard. "Uhhhhhh! Shit. Unn. Unn. Unn." Her body shivered. She felt rivers of euphoria coursing through her body like a tidal wave.

Makaroni slurped her juices hungrily. He sucked all over her inner thighs. He left behind wet marks. Then he stood up and stroked his piece. It stood out from his belly like a mini baseball bat. "I want that pussy, mama. Make me take that box."

Cassidy opened her thighs as wide as she could. She peeled open her lips, exposing her pink. Two fingers snuck into her opening. "I need you, Makaroni. Mama need that dick, baby. Come give me some. Please." She placed a foot on the couch, and the other on the carpet. She pulled at her nipples. Her juices seeped into her ass crack.

Makaroni fell between her legs. He lined himself up, slid in. Her left calf was placed on his right shoulder. He slammed home and proceeded to fucking her as hard as he could, sucking one nipple, and then the other. "Uh. Uh. Uh. Uh. Cassidy. Uh. Shit, ma. Fuck!"

She kept her mouth wide open while he long-stroked her deeper and deeper. Her insides were scorching. They felt tight. He could feel her working her pussy muscles. She was so good at that. It was another reason Makaroni loved vet pussy. Older women knew how to work their insides. They knew how to drive a man crazy, he thought.

Cassidy pulled him down and sucked his neck. She bit into it and ran her tongue over the bite marks. "Harder, baby. Fuck me harder." Her breathing was rugged.

Makaroni bounced up and down. Her pussy was so meaty. He couldn't believe how good it felt wrapped around his pipe. Her scent began to waft up to his nose. It encouraged him to beat it harder and faster. The couch tapped against the wall with each plunge.

Cassidy dug her nails into his big back. "Aw, fuck, baby! You so deep! You so deep, Makaroni!" She arched her back and came again.

Makaroni felt her pussy vibrating. That was too much for him. He cocked back and slammed forward, digging deep into her belly, cuming back to back. "Ma! Uh. Uh. Uhhhh. Un-uh!" He jerked, releasing his seed.

Cassidy held him between her thighs. She knew that he was cuming in her. Each jet splashed her walls. It sent a jolt of electricity through her. She hugged his body tighter. "That's my baby. Damn, I missed you."

Seth stood in the hallway in disbelief. Their love making had been so amorous that they had not even noticed that he'd been watching them for ten full minutes. He couldn't believe what he'd witnessed. He felt angry. He felt hurt. He felt like killing the both of them, but especially Makaroni. The young man had violated his wife. He had broken their covenant. He deserved death in his book, but so did Cassidy. He stood

frozen, not knowing what to do next. He felt like getting his gun and going crazy. He was so angry that he was shaking.

Cassidy straddled Makaroni's lap and slid him back into her box. She sunk down on him, riding slow while she held his shoulders. "Mmm. Mmm. Mmm. I missed you."

Makaroni held her ass. He rubbed all over her back. Her titties bounced. The nipples were fully erect. His tongue licked them in circles. "I missed you too." Makaroni didn't know if he was being honest with her. He didn't know how to really feel about Cassidy. He'd grown up under her and he had always saw her as a second mother. He cared about her. He wanted to protect her, and there was no doubt that he lusted after her for majority of his life. She had always been super sexy and strapped in his book. But as far as feelings, he didn't think he had any of those for her on that level.

Cassidy rode him faster, looking into his eyes. His hard pole lunged inside of her and knocked at her G spot over and over. That young dick was amazing to her. Makaroni was more than forbidden fruit. She knew if they had ever gotten caught doing what they were doing that all hell would break lose. Stevo was a lunatic, and Seth could be one as well. Every time she felt Makaroni go deeper, a spark would go of inside of her. She knew it was wrong, but for her that is what made it so right. She pressed her chest into his face and allowed for him to feast upon her nipples.

Makaroni gripped her ass and pulled her into him again and again. He sucked hard on her right nipple and came again. He humped up into her. "Mmm. Mmm. Mmm."

Cassidy closed her eyes with a smile on her face. "Yeah, honey. Mmm, yeah. I love it." She wrapped her arms around his neck and kissed his lips. "You make me so happy, Makaroni. I swear I mean that." She rested her head on his shoulder. "You make me feel like a little girl again."

Makaroni was taken off guard by that statement. He didn't know how to feel about it. His piece was still hard and connected inside of her. "Don't go catching feelings now, ma. You already know I love you, but we just doing our thing. Can't go past that."

Cassidy sat up. "Oh, I know, baby. I know. That still shouldn't stop you from holding me though." She kissed his cheek. "We good though. I know you got me, baby." Cassidy felt emotions that she knew were dangerous. She tried to ignore them, but they were strongly present.

Seth aimed his gun at the pair. He had a mug on his face. He imagined squeezing the trigger and sending them both to hell. How could Cassidy betray him were his most reoccurring thoughts. How could Makaroni fuck his wife? He would make them both pay. He promised this to himself. He lowered his gun and eased out of the hallway.

Ghost

Chapter 5

Two months passed. Makaroni and Stevo were able to acquire three more Trap houses with the help of Sheryl and her connections. Makaroni and Stevo worked tirelessly grinding in the Traps. They worked from sunup to sundown. They only rested for a few hours a piece then they were right back to working the Rebirth as if it were going out of style. JaMichael kept the shipments coming. As soon as they would sell out, early the next morning JaMichael would have a delivery car pull up with bricks of the Rebirth hidden inside of it. In return, Makaroni would UPS JaMichael boxes of money that had been double wrapped. When JaMichael received the shipment of funds, he sent Makaroni a coded text that allowed for Makaroni to know that he had received everything. They ran a smooth operation, and the money began to come at a fast pace for both Makaroni and Stevo so much so that they felt like they needed to hire extra help.

A week after Makaroni and Cassidy had been together, Stevo came back from a trip that he had taken to Chicago with a group of teenagers. He pulled his Chevy Blazer up beside Makaroni's Eddie Bauer truck just as Makaroni was about to get out of it. He rolled down the window and stuck his head out of it. "Say, bruh, it's a few ma'fuckas that I want you to meet."

Makaroni adjusted the Mach. 11 on his lap. He looked over to Stevo's trucks and the first thing he noticed was that it looked packed. In the passenger's seat sat a young dude with long dread locks and a blue bandana over his face. The back of Stevo's truck was more of the same. Five other dudes. Their faces were covered in the same fashion. "Who is all of those niggas?"

49

Stevo smiled. He was high as a kite off of Mollie and Percocet. "That's what I wanted to talk to you about. I took a trip down to the Land and scooped up a bunch of starving killas from the Village. These my lil' young niggas. They finna ride under me on this Stevo Gang shit." He looked back at his Hittas and nodded. Then back out to Makaroni.

"Stevo Gang? What the fuck you talking 'bout? Nigga, we get money. We ain't on all of that banging shit. We can't get rich and fall under somebody else."

"I ain't somebody else. Nigga, I'm saying that I'm the head. These niggas finna fall under me. That's how that shit finna go. I'm finna put them up in the Traps over on Vliet and Wells. We finna sew the blocks up. How you feel about that?" He sipped from a bottle of Cristal. The suds ran down his throat and tickled his stomach.

Makaroni waved him off. "Do what you do. I'm working on Seventeenth and Eighteenth off of West North Avenue. Sheryl just got me two more spots over that way. I got a few of the lil' homies from out that way that know the hood to work my shit. I'm finna head over there to see what's good right now."

Stevo held up a finger. He pulled his Blazer to the curb and parked it. Then he came across the street with a blunt in his right fingers, and a bottle of Cristal in his other hand.

Makaroni jumped out of his truck and met him halfway. "Nigga, you tripping."

Stevo shook his head. "I ain't never tripping. We getting a lil' money now. We supposed to go back to the ghetto that we came from to cop our project niggas. You can't trust these Milwaukee ma'fuckas. Most of them are snitching. The other half is sheisty and always on some bullshit. Breed n'em on that same shit. The fellas back home giving me a slot up here long as I keep them dues coming back home every other week.

That's dues for me, and for every one of these lil' niggas that I'm taking under my wing. It's a win-win. We get cold hearted, hungry killas for the low. Killas that believe in and stick to loyalty. Killas that honor me as head that's finna crush these Milwaukee niggas. You can't ask for a better deal. It's time we move these ma'fuckas around in this city anyway."

Makaroni mugged the truck behind Stevo. He saw how the group of killas eyed him with piercing eyes. He didn't get a good feeling from them. "Nigga, we been out here trapping for months on end by ourselves. Now you feeling like you wanna branch out back to Chicago and get them mobs involved? Are you serious?"

Stevo nodded. "As a heart attack. Look, dis what I'm finna do. I really don't care what you do with your side of our shit. I can say this though. I'll bet you in a months' time that our revenue doubles because of what I'm finna do. Can you say the same thing?" He took a puff from his stuffed blunt. The smoke was harsh. It boosted his high immediately. His eyelids were low.

Makaroni was quiet for a second. He didn't understand what was getting into Stevo. "Bruh, why it seem like we doing our own shit all of the sudden? What happened to us handling this business together?"

"I'm still with you one hundred percent. I'm just ready to get some serious dough. It's time we turn this ma'fucka into the Windy. We getting that bag, but we could be getting a lot more paper if we did shit the Chiraq way." Chiraq was what most of the locals called Chicago because of its bloody wars, and constant feuding within itself.

"Aiight then. You do what you gotta do on your end, and I'ma handle this business on dis side. Like I said, I'm finna go check out Seventeenth and Eighteenth off of West North Avenue. I'ma get some shit put together over that way. It's a lot

of fiends moving up from the eastside, and they are settling right into the area over that way. It's destined to be a cash cow real soon. It's important for us to capitalize off it like ASAP."

"Well, nigga, I support you. Do what you gotta. That's what I'ma do. I don't give a fuck what nobody say." He drank from his Cristal again. "Anyway, I'ma fuck wit' you in a minute. I got a few moves to make." He got back into his Blazer and skirted away from the curb.

Makaroni stood looking dumbfounded. Stevo had never acted so funny toward him. He wondered what was going on inside of his homeboy, but he didn't have time to dwell on it. He had to get to the northside in the interest of business.

***

Later that night Keaira climbed into Stevo's truck with an attitude. He was more than four hours late picking her up. He'd told her that he was going to scoop her at seven o'clock so they could have a nice dinner out. But it was eleven-thirty at night and he was just making it to her place. She was irritated. She slammed the door to his truck. "Damn. What the fuck took you so long?"

Stevo pulled away from the curb. "Bitch, don't start all that arguing and bickering shit. I had a few moves I had to buss before I got to yo ass. I'm here now though. Be grateful for that."

She crossed her arms. "Stevo, I'm so tired of this shit. I swear to God I am."

"Bitch, tired of what? A ma'fucka hitting yo hand every fuckin' day? My son got a whole new wardrobe. Your bills paid. What the fuck more do you want from me?"

"What about your respect? I am the mother of your son. You ever thought about giving me that? Huh?"

"Here we go with this shit. It's like ain't no winning wit' yo ass, no matter what I do. On some real shit though Keaira, it ain't for me to respect you. You ain't my bitch. I ain't tryna fuck with you on that level. I'm in these streets, and its way too many bitches for me to be settling down with just one. Especially yo ungrateful ass."

"Ungrateful? How am I ungrateful? Because I asked you to show me some respect? That makes me ungrateful?"

Stevo mugged her. "Bitch, you ungrateful because all you care about is yo self. I been out here risking my ma'fuckin' life to make shit happen while you been at home sitting on yo ass. Instead of you coming at me on some laid-back shit, you always got a ma'fuckin' attitude. That shit get old just like the same pussy do."

Keaira didn't know what to say. She was accustomed to Stevo's bad mouth and thuggish ways. She didn't know what she expected from him now that he was stepping up to the plate financially. His attitude seemed worst. He acted more irritable toward her. It made her feel low. "Look, Stevo, I'm sorry if I been getting on your nerves. I guess I been feeling that since you are getting money now that maybe you, me and our son can finally be a family now. I just didn't know how to approach you about that. But after hearing what you said about so many other women being out there, and the same pussy getting old, I guess it is what it is."

He shrugged. "That's fucked up for you. I don't feel shit. You wasn't trying to holler that family shit when I was broke, bitch. I don't wanna hear that shit now. I'ma keep hitting yo hand. You gon' keep spending that shit on my son, and occasionally yourself. I don't wanna be with you. I fuck with bad young hoez only. That's just that. No old bitches allowed." He wasn't purposely trying to offend her. He was being honest and trying his best to let her know how he felt.

"I'm only twenty-one. That ain't old."

"N'all it ain't, but you are old news in general. Matter fact." He pulled the truck to the side of the street. He pulled out a knot of hundred-dollar bills. Peeled one off and handed it to Keaira. "Huh, bitch. Get the fuck out of my truck."

Her eyes bugged out of her head. "What?" She looked down the street and saw the Metrolink bus ten blocks down. That bus would drop her off a block away from her house. "You really finna put me out?"

"You getting on my ma'fuckin' nerves, Keaira. I don't feel like dealing with you right now. So, yeah, get the fuck out of my truck."

Keaira shook her head. "Why would you have me kill somebody if you didn't give a fuck about me. That man that you had me kill loved me, and he took to Steven. If you knew that you were going to kick me to the curb as soon as you got your weight up, then why you didn't let me be happy with him?"

"I don't know what the fuck you talking about." He lied. "But get out of my shit though. Take that hundred-dollar bill and buy yourself something that will make you happy. 'Cause I can't make you happy, and I don't want to. Bye."

Keaira felt tears pour down her cheeks. "One day you gon' get yours, Stevo. All of this hurt that you press upon people. All of this tragedy. One day God is gon' get yo ass back."

He grabbed her with blazing speed around the throat and slammed her to the passenger's door. "Bitch, fuck you. I don't give a fuck about this shit you talking. If God get me, then He do. It is what it is. Fuck this world and every ma'fucka in it. I was sent here to hurt ma'fuckas. I was sent here to destroy. Bitch, I am the Reaper." He pulled the handle on the door and pushed her into the street. "Get yo broke ass on the bus." He laughed and stormed away from her.

Keaira fell to her knees in the street, scraping them. She felt like shit. She had never been treated so unfairly in her life. What made matters even worst was that she had a son by Stevo. Yet she felt like he treated her as if he hated her. She slowly got to her feet and jogged to the bus stop just has the Metrolink bus pulled up, sounding like a big soda pop had been opened. *Ka-szzzz!* The only thing on her mind was to get rid of Stevo. She was tired of him making her feel lower than scum. Tired of him crapping on her. She wanted to hurt him worse than he had ever been hurt before in his life. Then she would get rid of him for good. She settled into the city bus's seat with a smile on her face. Hell hath no fury like a woman scorned. Soon she promised herself that Stevo would find that to be true.

***

Stevo pulled up in front of Kandace fifteen minutes later. She climbed into the truck. Stevo already had his dick out of his jeans. "Bitch, close that door. We finna take a ride and you gon' top me off. You cool with that?"

She nodded. "Yeah."

"Say, 'Yeah, daddy'."

"Yeah, daddy." She settled to her knees and took ahold of her sister's baby daddy's dick. She stroked it for a minute, then slid it into her mouth with her eyes closed.

Stevo wrapped his fingers into her hair to help guide her. He pulled away from the curb while she went to work on him. It felt good as soon as she got to going. "Mmm. You been gathering up yo friends like I told you?"

Kandace popped him out with a loud sucking noise. She looked up to him. "Yeah, I got three of them that are willing to get down for you. They ready to run away from home and do whatever it takes to make some paper. They say they are tired of being broke. Two of them just graduated from high

55

school, too. They wanna go to college, but their parents are too broke to send them. I told them that you could help them get their money up, and then they could send themselves. They liked the sound of that." She sucked him back into her mouth, moaning all around his piece. She popped it back out after two minutes. It rested against her jaw. "Even when they officially sign under you, that won't mean that you are going to kick me to the curb, does it, Stevo?"

Stevo shook his head. "N'all, baby. That's gon' mean that you are going to become my bottom bitch. I'll never forget that you was with me when all of this got started. I promise you that." Stevo felt that he had to say what he knew Kandace wanted to hear. He was going to use her as bait to reel in other females her age. He knew that there were large sums of money in the pussy industry. He wanted his slice of that pie and he had every bit of intention of riding Kandace down that proverbial highway. He didn't care that she was Keaira's little sister. It was all about those dollars.

Kandace sucked his dick hard. She took as much of him as she could. She wanted to please him. She felt that if she did, she would never have to worry about feeling the struggle again. The thought of having her own money and being able to buy whatever she wanted was so appealing to her that she was willing to do anything to live that life. Even if it meant betraying her sister.

"Yeah, baby, Daddy gon' get you right. You belong to me now. Just keep doing what I tell you. Awright?"

She popped him out. "Okay." Then she got right back to sucking.

Chapter 6

After two months of setting up shop and hustling as hard as he could, Makaroni finally had North Avenue popping hard. He invaded the blocks of Fourteenth and North Avenue, all the way up to Twenty-First and North Avenue. He flooded the area with the Rebirth. Instead of going to war over turf, he invited the local Dope Boys to work under him. Months prior to him arriving on the scene they had been getting product that was less than thirty percent. Dope feinds were driving all the way to Chicago just to get their fixes. The area was losing money fast.

The Dope Boys from Fifteenth and Sixteenth Streets came together and had a meeting about Makaroni on whether they were going to allow for him to enter into their hood and get money, or if they were going to run him off of their blocks. When Makaroni proposed that for each kilo that they got rid of he would supply them with nine zips of the Rebirth as payment, there was nothing else to be talked about. They agreed to let him have two houses as Traps on each of their blocks. It took two weeks, and the other block leaders followed suit, and thereby allowing for Makaroni's growth and expansion.

In three months, all of the Dope Boys in the area were getting twice as much money as they were before. They owed it all to Makaroni. They pledged their undying loyalty to him. Most were willing to die for him with no hesitation. This gave Makaroni confidence to continue investing in their community, and their soldiers.

Stevo was taking care of business in a different way. He didn't care about negotiations or having sit-downs. He was all about the bloodshed and bullying his way into the Dope Game. One week after Makaroni took over Twenty-First and North Avenue. Stevo saw where his right-hand man's success

was headed, and he became jealous. He had his troops gather in the basement of one of his Trap houses on Twenty-Fifth and Kilbourne. He sat at the head of the table with a mug on his face, and a plate of the Rebirth in front of him. He made four lines and tooted one hard. In doing so he broke one of Rubio Flores's golden rules. Never use the Rebirth. Using the Rebirth was punishable by death. The Cartel leader swore that fate. Stevo didn't care. He took a second line and felt like cuming in his pants. The Rebirth had him feeling murderous and euphoric all at the same time. He pushed the plate away and rubbed his nose. His eyes were as red as fireballs.

The basement was packed with a bunch of low-life hustlers and killas that looked up to Stevo as if he were a young god. He was the one putting food on their tables. He put clothes on their backs. And it was because of him that these hustlers were fucking some of the baddest females in the city. They honored him in blood.

Stevo sat the assault rifle in his lap. He slammed a magazine inside of it and looked over the crowded room. "We on business tonight, kinfolks. Ma'fuckas finna feel this steel."

DaBaby was a dark skinned, slightly heavyset, young killa with the angelic face of a child. He had short curly hair, and a mouth full of gold. Back in Chicago he was known for killing at a young age. By twelve years old he'd already had ten bodies under his belt. "Mane, dem ma'fuckas could make shit a lot easier for themselves if they just jumped down with the fellas, but you know that we don't want shit easy no way. We wanna give they ass just what they looking for." He announced in his country accent.

Stevo was floating on air. "I want you to go in that ma'fucka tonight, baby boy, and make a statement for me. Let ma'fuckas know that we ain't wit' negotiations. We don't take no for an answer. We want that whole complex. All of

Highland. Since Domino ain't trying to give them bitches up, we gotta make a example out of his ass. It's as simple as that." Stevo closed his eyes and nodded out for a second.

DaBaby stood up and stepped beside him. "Check dis out, Mane. This move here is on me. I'm in charge of dis shit tonight, so y'all gon' do what I say. It's as simple as that." He looked around the room. "Anybody object?"

The room was quiet. His record was well known. He may have been one of the youngest soldiers in the room at fifteen years old, but he was respected highly, second to Stevo.

Stevo opened his eyes. "Y'all go over there to Highland and make that bitch red with blood. When you get back, we flying out to Vegas to celebrate our victory. Every thang on me. Guns up." He held the assault rifle in the air. The entire room took out their weapons and held them in the air. "No mercy?"

"No mercy!" They all hollered in unison.

***

Keaira stepped up to Maisey's front door and rang the doorbell. She felt nervous about what she was about to do. But she was desperate. She looked over her shoulder and saw that Makaroni's Eddie Bauer truck was parked in front of his mother's home. She was hoping that he wasn't busy. That he would give her a few minutes of his time.

Maisey peeked out of the window and saw Keaira standing on the porch. She was holding Steven's little hand. She smiled and opened the door, happy to see them. "Hey, girl. What brings you over here?" She asked leaning down and picking the two-year-old Steven up. He was bundled up in his little Jordan jacket and winter hat. Keaira had placed a scarf around him as well.

"I need to talk to Makaroni. It's urgent. I feel a little bit lost. I don't know what to do right now." She said, feeling on the verge of tears.

Maisey felt bad for her. "What's the matter? Is it anything that I can help you with?" She grabbed a hold of her hand and helped her inside.

Keaira shook her head. "No, mama. I wish you could. The only person that could help me is Makaroni right now. Is he busy?"

She shrugged. "I don't know. You are more than welcome to go in there and see though." She kissed Steven's cheeks. "I'll keep his handsome self company while you do that. Won't I, baby? Won't I?" She asked him, nuzzling into his neck.

Steven busted up laughing. "No."

Keaira hugged half of Maisey. "Thank you, mama. Where is he at?"

"In his old room, last I checked. Gone in there and tell him I sent you if he give you a hard time." Maisey waved her in that direction.

Keaira took a deep breath and headed down the hallway that led to Makaroni's old room. When she stepped in front of his closed doors, she knocked on it. She had butterflies in her stomach.

Makaroni had been counting money for an hour straight. He had fifty thousand dollars in cash in neat piles of ten thousands lined up on the bed. "Who is it?" He had sixty more thousand to count. "I gotta get me a money machine." He said out loud.

"It's Keaira, Makaroni. I need to talk to you for a minute."

"Shorty, I'm on something in here. Hit me up on Facebook later a something." He definitely didn't feel like getting involved with Keaira. He already knew that if she was hitting

him up that it had something to do with Stevo and their relationship. That wasn't his business.

"Makaroni, please. I'm losing my mind." Keaira felt like she was on the verge of breaking down.

He got up and answered the door. "What up, shorty?" He moved back. "Come on in." He sat on the bed and picked up a stack of cash, counting.

Keaira saw all of the money and couldn't believe her eyes. Her gold-digger instincts kicked in right away. She had forgotten which angle she was about to play on Makaroni now. She wanted to get her hands on some of the cash she saw before her.

"Yo, close that door. I'm letting yo ass know right now that if you finna come crying to me about what Stevo done did, I'm finna put yo ass out. Y'all business is y'all business, not mine."

Keaira knew that Makaroni had more compassion between the two. She fell to her knees and covered her face. She forced tears to come out of her eyes. "I can't take this shit no more. I'm ready to kill myself." She cried.

Makaroni looked down at her. He sat the money aside. "Fuck is you talking about?"

She cried harder. "He ain't doing nothing for us. We struggling. I'm tired of him putting his hands on me. I try so hard to be a good woman. Lord knows I do." She screamed into her hands to emphasize her point.

Makaroni knelt beside her and rubbed her back. "Damn. Shorty, quit all that crying. I got you. What type of money you need?"

Keaira smiled with her face covered. She made her voice shake. "I'm behind on the bills. Steven daycare fees are kicking my ass too. I ain't got no way to bring him back and forth. They done repossessed my car because the bill ain't been paid

since Stevo made me do what he did." She turned around and buried her face into his chest. "I can't do this anymore."

Makaroni felt sorry for her. He held her tighter. "Look, I'ma hit yo hand, and help you with them bills. Don't tell Stevo though. I don't want him thinking I'm stepping on his toes or somethin'."

"I ain't gon' tell him nothing. I appreciate you so much, Makaroni. I know you ain't gotta help me out. But thank God you are. It really means a lot to me." She kissed his cheek and rested her head on his shoulder.

Makaroni felt like Stevo needed his ass whipped. They were finally making a way for themselves. He felt that Stevo should have been taking care of his responsibilities as a man. The streets were supposed to be secondary. He didn't understand him, and never had. But he was still his right hand. Loyalty was everything to Makaroni.

***

It was one o'clock in the morning on a chilly Thursday night. A masked DaBaby hunched down in the Highland Apartments complex parking lot with a sawed-off double barrel shotgun in his hands. The sounds of Moneybagg banged out of a car's speakers loudly. The bass caused the ground to vibrate. DaBaby rushed across the gravel with two killas following his path. Three more ran into the apartment building door in search of Domino's hustlers. DaBaby hurried across the lot. He stopped on the side of the car that was banging the loud music. He crept alongside of it. When he got by the driver's side he popped up with the weapon in his hand. He aimed it at Domino's brother that sat nodding to the music.

In the passenger's seat was Domino's daughter's mother. She was rolling a blunt laced with powder cocaine. DaBaby fired the double barrel. The slugs shot from the short barrel of

the gun and knocked half of Domino's brother's face off. The pieces landed against the windshield along with blood and bone painting it red.

Domino's baby's mother screamed. "Ahh! Ahh! Please! Please!" She held her hands up. She looked back down to the dead man in the passenger's seat and broke into a fit of screams again.

"Bitch, shut up before I blast yo ass. Where is Domino?" DaBaby roared.

She pointed toward the building. "He upstairs with our daughter. Please don't hurt her. She's just a baby. Whatever he did, it ain't got nothing to do with us."

"Bitch, shut up. What apartment is he in?" DaBaby asked.

"Two-B. Go right up the steps. First door to your left. Just please don't hurt my—" She began.

Boom! Chick-chick. Boom! DaBaby jumped back as her noodles splashed out of the window. Tiny specks of brain matter stuck to his clothes. He could smell the scent of her burnt flesh. He pulled the shotgun out of the window with it smoking.

Minutes later he loafed on the side of apartment 2B with four of his goons. He had two on each side of the door. He took a step back and kicked it in with one try. His goons invaded the apartment on business. Chaos ensued. DaBaby waited in the hallway until it sounded like his goons had things under wraps. Then he walked inside and was met with the sights of a bound Domino. Three of Domino's men were laid face-down on the carpet. They had assault rifles pointed to the back of their heads.

DaBaby walked up to Domino and pulled his mask off of his face. "Nigga, you see my face? Huh?"

Domino closed his eyes tight. "N'all, nigga. I ain't seen shit." He knew what it meant if you seen Dababy's face. It

meant that you would never breathe another breath. "What do you want? I got ten pounds in this ma'fucka. You can have every thang."

DaBaby could hear a child crying in the back room. Most would've felt sympathy for taking the life of a parent, especially with the child crying in the backroom, but DaBaby felt nothing. He pressed the barrel of the shotgun to Dominos forehead. "My homie said he wanted this complex. You had to make shit difficult. Y'all ain't getting no real money up out dis ma'fucka anyway."

"He can have it. Fuck Highland. He can have this bitch." Domino said, trying to cop a plea.

"N'all, nigga, you already know what it means when I show up. Stevo gang-gang!" *Boom!* A single shot completely decapitated Domino. He fell backward in the chair. "Murk all of them."

Shots went off all around the room. Gunsmoke filled the air mixed with the scent of burnt flesh and blood. Dababy's troops raided the Trap house and took everything that Domino had stashed. They left the Trap looking like it had been hit by a tornado, and with the baby screaming at the top of its lungs.

Chapter 7

Montana rolled into town in the first week of February. It was already sixty degrees out, warm and sunny. Montana was rolling a bright pink Lexus truck. She pulled up to the curb of Maisey's house and jumped out fitted in tight Prada pants, a Prada blouse, with red-bottomed heels. She ran to her mother and gave her a big hug. "Man, mama, I missed you so much." She hugged her tighter.

Maisey had tears in her eyes. She hadn't seen her daughter in months. She looked so much older to her. She appeared well put together. She had put on a few pounds that complimented her beauty. "Girl, why did it take you so long to come and visit me?"

Montana felt sad. "I know, mama, but I had to get myself established down there. Now, I got me a hair salon and half of a dance club. I'm going to school. I'm doing alright for myself. I'm still sorry though." She hugged her mother again.

"It's okay, baby. I understand. Mama really do."

Makaroni stepped out of the house with two gold chains around his neck. He had a big diamond in each ear, and rocked Chanel from his chest to his Balenciaga shoes. "I know that ain't my lil' sister right there!" He hollered, walking down the steps.

Montana saw him and took off running in her heels. She met him halfway. Her arms wrapped around his body. "Dang, boy, I missed you."

Makaroni kissed her cheek. "I done missed you, too. It feel good to finally see you. You smell good as hell."

She took a step back and looked into his eyes. "I been going nuts missing you, Mack. You know what I'm talking about, too."

He laughed. "You tripping. You see mama right there."

Maisey walked up. "Yeah, don't leave me out. I wanna know what she talking about." She looked from her daughter to her son.

Montana blushed. "It's a sibling thing, mama. No offense."

Maisey shrugged. "Well, I guess. I'ma let y'all gon' 'head and catch up. Montana, I'm almost done cooking all of your favorites. Don't go too far." Maisey headed in the house.

"I won't." Montana promised. She watched her mother until she disappeared inside.

Makaroni peeped how she was fitting those jeans. Her ass was poked out further than he remembered. "Damn, sis, you done got thick as hell. Where all of that ass come from?"

Montana smiled over her shoulder at him. "We need to take a drive so we can catch up. Come on. You can feel how this Lexus roll." She walked to her truck and popped the locks.

Makaroni followed behind. His eyes never came from her ass. He could only imagine how soft it felt. He couldn't wait until they left their mother's block. "I'm finna run inside and tell mama we finna roll out for a minute and that we'll be back. Cool?"

"Cool."

***

Keaira sat across from Stevo at her apartment as he played with their son Steven. She had so many devious things going through her mind that it was making it hard for her to think. She was seriously irritated because she knew that Stevo wasn't going to stay long. He had five females waiting for him inside of his truck that was parked in the front of her place. Whenever she thought that it was impossible for him to disrespect her worst than he had previously, he always came up with a new way.

Stevo laughed at Steven attempting to dance a little. He glanced over to Keaira and saw that she was mugging him. He grunted. "Shorty, what's yo problem?"

She shook her head. She didn't want to fight. "Nothing. I was just looking at you, that's all." She looked down to Steven. "Are you still gon' take him shopping for shoes and stuff?"

"That's all yo ass care about. You don't even make that shit a secret either. You obvious as a muthafucka." He shook his head in disgust. "When you gon' get yo ass up and make a living? You think just 'cause you my baby mama that I'm gon' support yo ass for the rest of yo life?"

Keaira felt offended. She could never ask him a simple question without it leading to an insult from him. "I'm looking for a job. Don't worry, I'll be straight in a minute."

"Bitch, you need to come work for me."

"Work for you where? Selling dope? Boy, please." She rolled her eyes.

"Ain't nobody said shit about selling no dope. It's other ways for females to get money." He snickered.

"How?" She was oblivious to his insinuations.

"Shid, I'm finna open a strip club on Fondulac. You could work in there and get yo money up. You still working wit' a lil' something that these thirsty ass niggas out here might wanna see. Long as you keep the stretch marks covered up."

She jerked her head back. "Nigga, first of all, I only got a few. Secondly, you would let the mother of yo child work in a strip club? Fuck type of nigga is you?"

"Bitch, you ain't gotta dance. You could be a bartender. Ever thought about that?"

Keaira waved him off. "I'd never degrade myself like that. Miss me with that talk. Awright." She bent over and picked

up Steven. "You should have a lot more respect for me than you do. I don't understand why you hate me so much."

"I don't. This just how I am. You a bum bitch. I treat bum hoez like they need to be treated. Only difference with you is that I'm trying to give you a gateway to some serious paper. Yo punk ass too stubborn to see that." He stood up and pulled out five hundred dollars in ones, fives, tens and twenties. He threw it into her face, causing the money to explode all over the living room. "Here. That should be enough to get my son what he need. Don't be buying him none of that cheap shit either."

Keaira stood still. She felt like shit once again. He had degraded her and crapped on her in front of their son. She felt like breaking down crying. She tried her best to keep her composure.

Stevo laughed. "Let me leave before you get to crying and shit. I'll holler at you when I feel like it. Later." He left her apartment and slammed the door so hard that Steven started crying.

***

"Montana, you tripping. Damn, girl, mama live two blocks over. At least let's get a room or something." Makaroni advised.

Montana wasn't trying to hear nothing that he was saying. She took the keys out of the ignition and dropped them into her Hermes bag. Then she was straddling Makaroni's lap. She looked into his eyes. "I ain't let no nigga touch me since the last time you and I did our thing. And JaMichael been trying every single day. That boy act like he's obsessed with me." She sucked on Makaroni's neck. "How about you?"

He laughed. "I fucked a few hoez. Nothing serious. You know how dope boys do it." He gripped her ass. "Man, you

68

done got so thick that I wanna enjoy this pussy. I ain't trying to waste my first fuck in a truck. Hell n'all."

Montana licked the side of his neck. "I want you right now, big bruh. I don't think I can wait until tonight. Plus, mama reminding me of how wrong this really is. She making me feel guilty. What about you?"

Makaroni snuck his hand under her Prada blouse and played with her titties. Her hard nipples poked against his palms. "Look, we done already fucked. What's done is done. We can't unfuck, so it is what it is. Now that you done got this thick, I damn sure ain't finna pass up this pussy. Yo shit fye, too."

She giggled. "Shut up." She took a hold of his face and kissed him softly at first. He returned her kisses. Then her tongue slipped into his mouth. They began to make out loudly in the truck. Montana got wet immediately.

Makaroni pinched and pulled on her nipples. He squeezed her globes. They felt warm and hefty. "I'm fucking you tonight, Montana. Let's just go and have dinner wit' mama. Den once she happy we can spin off and do our own thing. How about that?"

She was breathing hard. "You can't even let me ride you for ten minutes? I just wanna feel yo dick in me. I been feening for it."

Makaroni got hard. His piece started to jump in his Chanel pants. "Damn, you making this shit hard." He unbuttoned her pants and slid his fingers into her panties. As soon as he felt her hot lips, his will power grew weaker.

"Mmm, bruh. Please fuck me real fast. We ain't even gotta go that hard." She groaned, opening her thighs for him.

Makaroni slid his fingers deep into her pussy. He pulled the digits out and sucked them into his mouth. She tasted sweet to him. "N'all, I wanna enjoy this pussy. You gotta let

me do that. Mama did a lot of cooking for you. We gon' eat up, and then big bruh gon' eat you. That's how that's finna go. Now, let's roll."

Montana was pissed, but she understood. "Okay, but you better fuck me good tonight. If I ain't climbing the walls then I'm ending our taboo thing. I mean that shit." She pulled out his dick and sucked it into her mouth for ten quick sucks. As soon as he started groaning, she pulled her mouth off of it, leaving him squirming. "Now, you feel like I feel."

***

The doorbell rang three times, jolting Keaira to her feet. She stepped in front of the full length mirror and gave herself a once over. She had to make sure that she was looking good enough to eat if she wanted her plan to take off in the right direction. She opened the silk robe and flashed her red negligee. The hem was so short that you could make out the lips of her pussy. She took a deep breath and stepped out of the mirror. She buzzed the door and waited. She hurried back to the mirror to look at herself one last time. She gave herself her stamp of approval just as knocks came on the door. She exhaled and turned the knob.

Stacy stood before her with a smile on his face. He'd just gotten out of the county jail after serving four months fighting a dope case that he took probation for. He was hot and horny. "Damn, shorty, you look good as a muthafucka." He eyed her from head to toe. "I see what you got on yo mind. Where that bitch ass nigga at?"

"That's who I wanna talk to you about. His punk ass gotta go. I'm willing to do anything to make that happen, too." She loosened the sash of her robe.

Stacy looked on hungrily. "Aiight. Cool, baby, but before we get into any of that, I gotta tear this ass up."

"Long as you promise to make getting rid of Stevo one of your first priorities now that you're home, you can do anything you want to me."

Stacy licked his lips. "I'm stanking that nigga and Makaroni anyway." He locked the door. "Let's get it in."

***

Montana couldn't take her eyes off of Makaroni the entire time they were eating Maisey's famous triple-cheesed lasagna. It didn't help that she popped two tablets of Mollie, and her clitoris was ultra-sensitive. Her mother asked her question after question. She answered them as fast as she could so that she could focus in on him. For some reason her body was calling out to him.

After an hour of eating and catching up, Maisey announced that she was tired. She yawned with her fists over her head. She kissed Montana on the cheek. Then she went around the table and gave Makaroni a hug and a kiss on the cheek. "Y'all, clean up my house before you lay down. Wrap up those leftovers. Cassidy said when she get back that she gon' want some. I'm sure that Seth will, too."

"Okay, mama." Montana said. She waited until she heard her door close before she rushed to Makaroni and threw her arms around his neck. She kissed his lips hard and bumped her pelvis into his front. "Come on, we finna do this right now. Fuck that hotel room." She whispered.

Makaroni squeezed her juicy ass. He kissed her lips and shivered from the feeling of taboo that coursed through him. There he was gripping Montana's backside and kissing her while Maisey was only a few rooms over. He knew it was wrong but something inside of him forced him to keep going.

Montana bit his neck. "You scared? Huh? What? You think you gon' get a whoopin' if we get caught a something?" She teased him.

Makaroni shivered again. "In yo room. I'm finna hit this pussy in yo room; bring back those play time memories. Come on." He scooped her up.

Chapter 8

Montana wrapped her thighs around his body. Makaroni carried her to her old room and kicked the door closed behind him. Montana continued to kiss all over his neck. Her tongue searched his ear canal as deep as it could go. She moaned so he could hear how riled up she was. "I always wanted you to fuck me in my room, Makaroni. I used to lay in the bed and think about you doing it to me every night when we were little." She kissed his lips again.

Makaroni fell to the bed with her. He was right between her legs. He ripped her blouse open and yanked her bra apart like a savage. Her breasts spilled out. He took them in his big hands and squeezed them together. "I remember when these first started coming in. I used to try and sneak up on yo ass just so I could see 'em. Yo nipples used to be poking through all of your shirts before you got that bra. I couldn't keep my hands off of myself. That's why every time we wrestled, I used to be squeezing them, and acting like that's how I fought." He sucked her left nipple into his mouth.

Montana arched her back. She thought that's what used to be happening back then, but she wasn't sure. She remembered every time they got done wrestling that her panties used to be soaked and she never understood why. She thought that something was wrong with her because she wasn't supposed to have been craving for Makaroni down there the way that she always had been. Now as he sucked her nipples, she had flashbacks on when they were little, and he used to be all over her while they play fought. He pulled her Pradas off her thighs, and to the floor. She felt his hand slide into her panties. He rubbed all over her sex lips, sucking her neck again.

"Remember how I used to rub your pussy through the panties while you acted like you was sleeping?" He bit into her neck. "Do you?"

Montana opened her thighs wider. She remembered those nights. They would wrestle for thirty minutes straight, playing Smackdown. Then Maisey would stop them, saying they were making too much noise. She would make them go into their own rooms. Makaroni would wait for a short time until he was sure Maisey was sleep. Then he would creep into Montana's room and slide into the bed with her, snuggling. Montana had a habit of laying on her back with her thighs wide open whenever she knew Makaroni was coming into her room. It never took Makaroni long before he was rubbing all over her box. His fingers never went into her panties out of fear of the unknown, but he would rub her box while she pretended to sleep until she came, unbeknownst to him.

"I remember." She whispered. "Ooo. I remember."

Makaroni pulled her panties to the side and slipped two fingers into her hot center. He stroked her while sucking her erect nipples. "I always wanted this pussy. Always. You so fine, Montana. Ain't nobody fucking wit' you. That's real." He sped up the pace.

Those words drove Montana crazy. She humped into his digits. "I want you. Unn. I want you, bruh. Please. Fuck me right now. Please." She could feel her juices pouring all over her ass cheeks.

Makaroni scooted down and sucked all over her thick inner thighs. He searched for her juices. Located them and slurped them up. His tongue made a path that led to her cat. Once there he pulled the material of her panties further to the side and exposed her engorged sex lips. He kissed them. He licked the length of them before he opened them wide to showcase her glossy pink. He sniffed. Shivered and stuck his

74

tongue as far into her as it could go. Then he traveled up and down the slit. His lips trapped her pearl tongue and sucked with enough force to drive Montana crazy.

She shook on the bed. She took a hold of his head and forced it into her middle. Her ankles came over his shoulders while he feasted on her delights. She moaned, cautious of Maisey in the other room. "Mmm, bruh. Mmm. I missed you."

Montana's scent was driving Makaroni crazy. His face was soaked with her juices. He flicked his tongue against her clit faster and faster. She bucked. Then she grabbed a pillow off of the bed and screamed into it, cuming hard. Makaroni blew on her clit and rubbed it from side to side as fast as he could. Before Montana could complete her first climax, another came rushing violently through her body. She bit the pillow and screamed.

Makaroni flipped her on to her stomach and opened her thick ass cheeks. He gripped the booty meat in each hand before his face was between her gap. His tongue invaded her crinkle, dipping into it over and over. His chin hairs brushed over her erect clitoris while he went to work on her back door. "This my pussy, Montana. I don't care what nobody say. This my shit right here." He darted his tongue in and out of her rosebud. His fingers dipped into her cat again. He finger-fucked her at full speed. Then he was sucking on her clit as if it were a nipple that produced milk.

Montana beat her fist on the bed. Tears came out of her eyes. It felt so good. The feeling was too much for her. She brought her right knee to her ribs and came again, screaming into the pillow. Her entire body shook as if she were having a seizure.

Makaroni flipped her back over and looked at her sexy body. He knew who she was to him and it heightened his sexual calling to her. Montana, in his mind, was the finest woman

he had ever seen. Her body was second to none. He sucked her nipples hard. Pinched and pulled on them until they were standing up like erasers. Then his tongue traced circles around her areolas. "You ready for me, Montana? Huh, sis?"

Montana could barely breathe. She was leaking between the legs. Her middle hurt. It ached for Makaroni. All she could do was open her thighs as wide as she could in answer to his question.

Makaroni positioned himself. He trailed the head of his big pipe up and down her slit. She was so wet that in a matter of seconds he was dripping with her juices. Her scent was heavy in the room. "Dis my pussy." He slid deep into her, inch by inch. He could feel the ridges of her womb as she enveloped him. When he was in as far as he could go, he leaned down and kissed her juicy lips.

Montana's eyes were stuck in the back of her head. She was filled to the max. His dick had her stuffed to capacity. She felt him licking all over her lips. He sucked the bottom one, and then the top, before his tongue made love to hers. Then he was sucking her nipples while his dick remained planted. She started to cry because the pleasure was so intense. Her nails dug into his back. "Fuck me, Makaroni. Please. Pipe me down."

Makaroni was obsessed with her D-cups. He brought his mouth away from the nipples and placed her left thigh on his shoulder. He started to long-stroke her, hitting the bottom with each stroke. Her cat seared him. The heat was intense. So intense that he stayed on the verge of cuming. He inhaled to keep her scent up his nostrils. The aroma of her pussy was like fuel to him. He sped up the pace and enjoyed her tightness.

Smack. Smack. Smack. Smack. Their skins collided again and again. Montana moaned. Sweat peppered her edges. She would have to get a touch-up first thing in the morning, but

she didn't care. The dick was so big. So good. So wrong, but right. "Unn. Unn. Bruh. Ooo. Mmm. Mmm. Mmm. Hit dis pussy. Hit it. Harder. Harder." She whimpered.

Makaroni went into overdrive, stabbing. He could hear her juices every time he stabbed into her. The bed squeaked with each thrust. The sounds drove him mad. He held her thigh firmer on his shoulder for leverage, fucking her like a stallion. "Dis my pussy. Mine!" He growled, feeling her work her inner muscles.

Cassidy came into Maisey's home and kicked off her heels. She reached down to massage her toes. "Damn, my feet hurt." She complained. She picked up her heels, making her way across the living room on stocking-clad feet. She stopped in the kitchen to see what Maisey cooked for dinner. She remembered texting her that she was going to make a lasagna because Montana was coming into town, and it was supposed to be her favorite. She opened the refrigerator and saw the glass dish right away with the aluminum foil over it. Her stomach growled. She thought about making her some when she heard Montana's moan. She bucked her eyes and closed the refrigerator. "I know Maisey ain't in there getting her groove back. Is she?" She asked out loud. She crept down the hallway and stopped outside of Maisey's door, placing her ear to it. All she heard was the sound of a fan. She held her breath to see if she would hear the moaning again.

After two minutes, she decided that it wasn't coming from her room. She walked back to the kitchen and stood still. She remembered seeing Makaroni's truck outside. She wondered if he'd brought a girl over. She shook that notion off. He had never done such a thing. The thought of it made her jealous. She had to clear her mind of that imagery. She was on her way back to the kitchen to fix her some late dinner when Montana moaned out loud again four times. Now, Cassidy was on the

case. She rushed down the hallway and stopped outside of Montana's room door. She placed her ear to it and sure enough she could hear both Makaroni and Montana grunting as they fucked each other with reckless abandon. Cassidy wondered what was going on the other side of the door. She could hear their skins slapping together. The creaking of the bed. One sniff and the aroma of sex was heavy to her nostrils. Curiosity was getting the better of her. She placed her hand on the doorknob and turned.

Makaroni pulled out of Montana and watched her crawl on all fours. He rubbed all over her ass. Her pussy was fat from the back. He rubbed it and opened the brown lips. He smacked her ass and slid his piece back into her. Grabbed her hips and proceeded to fucking her as fast and as hard as he could.

Montana lowered her face to the bed. She bit into the pillow, throwing her ass back at him. "Yes! Yes! Unn! Makaroni! Baby! Unn! Big bruh! Shit! Fuck me! Fuck me!"

Cassidy couldn't believe her eyes. Her pussy was soaked. Her juices ran down her thighs as she watched Makaroni pummel Montana like an animal. She couldn't understand how Montana was taking such a pounding. She wondered how it all began. Why it began. She pulled up her skirt and slipped her fingers into her own panties, going to town while she watched them in action from the doorway, unbeknownst to them.

"I'm finna cum, Mack. I'm finna cum again, Mack. Aww shit, big bruh." She slammed back on him with all her might ten hard times. When he poked her G-spot she came, falling on her stomach.

Makaroni stroked her twenty more times. Then he pulled out and came all over her ass cheeks in big globs. Montana reached behind herself and opened her cheeks for him. He didn't waste any time cuming in between them. Then he was

laying on top of her, sucking on the back of her neck, grinding into her ass.

Cassidy came fast on her knees. She pulled her fingers out of herself and crawled out of the room on shaky knees. She closed the door lightly behind her. She was still in disbelief by what she'd witnessed.

* * *

The next morning, Cassidy watched Montana and Makaroni making eyes at each other as they all sat at the breakfast table. Montana reached her foot under the table and placed it inside of Makaroni's lap while Maisey ate her foot to the right of her. Makaroni scooted forward just a bit so he could feet her pretty toes better. She mashed his piece over and over until it was nice and hard. Cassidy watched their expression and it drove her crazy. She couldn't wait to ask Makaroni how it all began between he and Montana.

"So, what did y'all do once I fell asleep last night?" Maisey asked.

Montana pulled her foot back, caught off guard by the questioning. "Just caught up a bit, mama. That's all." She snickered and spooned some French Toast into her mouth.

"Yeah, we just kicked back." Makaroni stood up. "I gotta go, though." He kissed Maisey on the cheek. "I love you, mama."

"I love you too, baby."

Montana followed him into the back room. "Where are you finna go? I thought we was gon' chill today."

"Aw, we is. I just gotta make some pickups on the money side. Then, I'm coming right back here so we can chill. Cool?"

She poked her bottom lip out. "I guess. Don't be all day though. You gon' have me missing you like crazy." She hugged him and kissed his lips.

Cassidy cleared her throat. "Uh, Mack, can I talk to you for a minute?"

Montana jumped from Makaroni and blushed. She looked back at Cassidy. "Don't be all day, Makaroni." She eased out of the room.

Cassidy closed the door and stepped into Makaroni's face. "So, when all of that start?" She looked into his eyes to see if he was going to be honest with her.

Makaroni turned his back to her and grabbed his coat. "What you talking about?" He wasn't sure how much she had seen.

Cassidy stepped around into his face. "Boy, don't play wit' me. I just seen that lil' girl kiss you on your lips. What? You think that's normal?" She continued to search his eyes. She could see that he felt guilty. She wondered if she should exploit it or not.

"That's my sister. A peck here and there. Don't mean nothing, ma. Fall back." He finished getting himself together.

Cassidy looked on, torn between telling him what she had sexually witnessed between him and Montana, or simply keeping the matter to herself. She didn't see any benefit either way. She was more curious as to when it all started. She waited until Makaroni got ready to leave the room before she blocked his path. "Look, baby, whatever y'all got going on ain't my business. I'm not going to make it my business either. The only thing I ask is that you don't lose sight of what you and I have. Can you promise me that?"

Makaroni looked down at her and smiled. "Cassidy, I don't know what you think me and Montana got going on, but I'm telling you that you are tripping. That's my baby sister. I love her. She give me a peck every now and then, and that's it. Far as you and I go." He pulled her to him and kissed her

80

on the forehead. "You already know that I got mad love and respect for you. That will never change."

Cassidy broke his embrace and pulled his head down. She kissed his lips aggressively, breathing heavily. Her hands rubbed up and down his back. When she broke their embrace, she was wet as a thunderstorm. "Don't forget about me, Makaroni. That's all I'm asking you." She stepped away from him and into the hallway, nearly bumping into Seth who was waiting outside of the door. She froze. "Hey, baby."

Seth looked her up and down, shaking. He glanced past her and to Makaroni. He saw the way that Makaroni's pants were poked out in the front, and this vexed him. He turned his back to Cassidy and walked off, plotting their murders.

Cassidy shrugged. "Don't forget what I said, Mack."

"I got you."

Ghost

Chapter 9

Two weeks later...

Stevo sat back on the love seat while Kandace and five of her young friends turned in a circle before him. He looked over their lingerie attire and nodded in approval. He had finally been able to secure a location in downtown Milwaukee that was close enough to the nightlife, but far away from the First District police station. He had six girls that were willing to do anything for him. Six bad bitches is what he called them, with Kandace being the promoter of him, and the one he used to keep the other five girls in line.

Stevo stood up and walked over to Kandace. He put his arm around her shoulder. His lips rested on her earlobe. "Baby girl, you know you making Daddy proud, don't you?"

Kandace nodded. "I hope so. I got five of the finest girls from my school. Four of them were on the cheerleading squad. Sasha, that's the red bone right there. She Puerto Rican and Black. That's her natural hair, and she down to do whatever for you. I think she gon' help us make the most money, daddy."

Stevo appraised Sasha. She was five feet three inches tall, a hundred and twenty-five pounds. She had short, curly hair, and a beautiful face. She reminded him of a prettier Selena Gomez. Her skin tone was golden. Her lips were juicy, and she spoke with a broken English accent. "Yeah, baby, I think you might be right." The other four girls ranged from caramel to chocolate. Each one was fine in their own right, with bodies to match their facial features. "Aiight, listen up. Tonight is the first night you hoez gon' be able to make some serious money. I know y'all tired of depending on yo parents to hit your pockets. Tired of not having yo own, so Daddy finna change all of

83

that. Everybody have a seat so I can give you some of this motivating powder." He ordered. He kissed Kandace on her lips and patted her ass. "You too, lil' baby."

Kandace took a seat and felt like the most special girl in the room. She had never seen Stevo kiss her sister on the lips. She remembered Keaira complaining about that. But every chance he got he was always kissing her lips. She felt that he really cared about her. Never having a strong male in her life before, Kandace was willing to do anything to gain and keep the love and support of Stevo. His attention and care was important to her.

Stevo grabbed an ounce of the Rebirth. He chopped through the tan powder that was on top of a golden platter with care. He'd chosen the platter because he was sure that the golden color of it would appeal to the young women. He knew at their ages appearance was everything. He took his time getting the Rebirth prepared. It felt grainy, and he could smell the stench of the chemicals coming off of it. He made twelve medium sized lines and sat back on the love seat. He rolled up a hundred-dollar bill. "Y'all see what I'm using for us to get lifted with? Huh? Daddy already got his money, right? Now, I want the same for you. If you just roll wit' me for three months, I promise to have you seeing more money than you have ever seen before. I'ma have my hoez rocking the latest of fashions. Everybody that has ever given you a hard time in life will be jealous. They gon' wish they could be a part of your circle, but that ain't how this shit works. We are a family. We live for each other. We ride for each other. We are supposed to be ready to die for each other. Do you bitches understand me?" He looked around the room and saw a bunch of nods. "Now, it's two lines on here for each one of you. Take them hard. Use this hundred-dollar bill to do so. As soon as you are done, I'ma want you to lean back with your eyes

closed and focus in on my voice. Take in every word that I'm saying. My muthafuckin' words are golden. You understand that?" Once again, each girl in the room nodded in agreement.

Kandace started with the golden platter. She placed it on her lap and picked up the hundred-dollar bill, placing it at the beginning of a line, and tooted hard. The Rebirth shot up her nasal canal and attacked her brain immediately. A sudden burst of euphoria took over her. She felt strong. She felt problem-free. She felt emotional, yet angry. The happy before it mellowed out and gave her the best feeling that she ever felt in her entire life. She closed her eyes and smiled.

"Take the other one, Kandace, and pass the platter." Stevo came over and ran his fingers through her hair.

"Okay, Daddy." She took the second line. Her heartbeat sped up. It pounded hard. Then the beats slowed all the way down. The euphoric feeling double timed. She felt wet between her thighs. Her clit came out of its hood in search of contact. She passed the platter to Sasha, who was sitting on the couch beside her.

Stevo stepped back and watched each girl take their lines. He nodded. He knew that nobody could resist the Rebirth. The person that controlled the Rebirth controlled the world. He was looking to make himself a millionaire off of the drug. He wanted to get as many people infected as he could. Powerful people that he could use as pawns in his rise to the top. Now he had seen a small sum of money he wanted more. He yearned for more power. He yearned to be a Kingpin.

After all of the girls had taken their lines, each one laid back on the couch with their eyes closed. Each were in their own zone. Far away from the confines of the ghetto. Miles away from heartache and pain. Each had a smile on their faces. It was the look that Stevo was hoping for. He picked up the platter. "Now, I got a few important men that are coming here

in just a few hours. Men that are going to make sure that all of us are eating the way we are supposed to. You bitches are my angels. We are on a mission to make a million dollars. Each and every one of you will play an intricate part in this rise. My expectations will be met. While it is my job to give you the world, I will not hesitate to get on yo ass when you screw up. I mean that."

The girls heard him loud and clear. They occasionally opened their eyes to see where he was as he spoke. The Rebirth prevented them from keeping their lids open for too long. Each of their middles were dripping with sexual fluid, yearning to be touched.

Stevo tested his method of control. He knelt in front of Sasha and rubbed her inner thigh. "How you feeling, baby?"

Sasha moaned, and opened her golden thighs wide. Her panties sunk into her sex lips. She shook. "I-I-I don't know." She quivered.

Stevo snuck his head between her legs. He kissed her right on the crotch and licked the material that covered the middle of her pussy. He sucked each exposed lip one after the other. Sasha brought her feet up to the pillows of the couch. Her pussy bussed wide open. Now the crotch band looked like a small strip that barely covered her gap. Her juices leaked out of her. She moaned and whimpered. She mentally begged for Stevo to touch her pussy for real.

Stevo stood up and looked down on her. "I see you ready to go, huh?"

She nodded. Usually shy, the Rebirth made her cast all of her inhibitions to the side. "I need you to touch me, Stevo."

Stevo grabbed a handful of her hair and yanked her head back. "Bitch, you think you earned the right to use my name? Huh?" He pulled harder on her hair.

"No. I'm sorry." The pulling of her hair was sending jolts to her clitoris. She loved having her hair pulled, but she knew that Stevo meant business. Common sense told her that.

"Who am I?" He asked.

"My daddy. You're Daddy." She whimpered with secretions leaking out of her. She prayed that he touched her soon or she was going to scream. The Rebirth had her sexual cravings ten times as bad as they had ever been. She felt out of control.

Stevo dove his hand between her thighs and pinched her clit. She yelped and came, screaming at the top of her lungs. "Bitch, don't you ever forget who I am. Get yo ass down and kiss my feet."

Sasha fell to her knees and kissed his Balenciaga runners. She was still shaking like crazy. "I'm sorry, Daddy. I will never make that mistake again. I promise."

Stevo mugged her. "Go sit yo ass down before I spank that ass."

Sasha hopped up. "Okay."

Carmen, a five-foot six inch, one-hundred-and-thirty-pound girl with brown eyes, and shoulder-length hair crossed her thighs as tight as she could. Her clit was driving her crazy. She imagined Stevo spanking her and wanted to cum. She wished that he would reach between her thighs and pinch her clit like he had done Sasha. She was starving for some physical contact from him. She squeezed her thighs again and shivered with her eyes closed tightly.

Stevo peeped her. He walked over to her and kneeled. "You Carmen, right?" He placed his hand on her knee.

Carmen moaned as a tremor ran through her clit. The Rebirth was taking full effect on her clitoris as it was with the other girls. "Yes." She opened her eyes.

He stroked her hair. "Baby, you heard what I desire from you, right?"

She nodded. "Yes."

"Yes, what?"

"Yes, Daddy."

Stevo smiled, looking into her eyes. He undid her thighs. He placed his hand beneath her gown and rubbed her naked pussy. He felt over the juicy lips. She was soaked and sticky. He could smell her heavy scent. He yanked her gown back and exposed her pussy. He opened it with his thumb and forefinger to eye her pinkness. Then his tongue attacked her like a savage.

Carmen started to moan loudly. It felt so good. She felt his tongue going in and out of her. His big lips sucked on her clit and sent her over the edge. She arched her back and came, bucking like a wild horse. "Ohhh! Ohhh! Ohhhhhhhh!" She screamed.

All around the room the other girls began to manipulate their kitties. Thick thighs were splayed wide open while their fingers went to work. The Rebirth caused them to go into overdrive. In a matter of five minutes each girl, with the exception of Carmen, were laid out on the floor on their backs, moaning and rubbing themselves furiously.

Stevo fingered Carmen at full speed while he sucked her clit. She wrapped her thighs around his neck and came back to back. She called out for him. Tears ran down her cheeks from the Rebirth-induced orgasm. The drug, along with Stevo, worked to conquer her in a way that her young mind didn't even know was possible. After she came again, Stevo stood up and wiped his mouth. "Awright, bitches. I'ma get this shit ready. Y'all finna take two more lines apiece and then our customers will be here. Make me proud. You earn my respect first, and then my love. Once you earn my love, there is

nothin' in this world that you can't have. Y'all belong to me. I'm gon' always take care of what's mine. Now, come give Daddy a hug."

They rushed him and all tried to hug him at once. They felt a sense of security with Stevo. They felt excited by the fear of the unknown. Each girl was ready for a new journey in life. A journey that they truly believed would lead to a lifetime of riches.

Stevo knew that mental manipulation ran the world. He hugged them with nothing but large sums of money on his mind. He refused to go back to struggling. He refused to be seen as anything less than a Boss. He was dead-set on using anybody and everything around him to reach the top. There was nothing that he would not do.

Ghost

Chapter 10

Two weeks after Cassidy caught Montana kissing Makaroni's lips, he was out trapping on 15th and North Avenue. Montana pulled up with Cassidy sitting in the passenger's seat of her truck. She honked her horn and pulled over to the curb in front of him. Montana hopped out and walked up to him.

It was a breezy Spring day. Most of the porches were filled in the neighborhood. Little kids rode their bikes up and down the block while yelling loudly. A few of the people had their radios out on their porches, blaring their music. Occasionally, a police car would cruise through to eye the residents, before they disappeared on to other pressing matters.

Makaroni hugged Montana. It took all of the willpower that he had to not squeeze her ass. Montana was wearing a tight, form fitting, knee length red and white Givenchy dress that made her body look tantalizing. She had her makeup done precisely. She smelled just as good to Makaroni. He squinted his eyes and shielded them with his hand to peep her passenger's seat. "What brings you out here, and who is that in the passenger's seat?"

Montana looked back to her truck. "Aw, that's Cassidy. I picked her up from work. I was gon' drop her off first, but I figured I should come and holler at you before I do anything else." She looked worried.

Makaroni picked up on it right away. He placed his arm around the small of her back. "What's the matter?"

Montana eyed the porch full of dope boys that worked under her brother. They watched her closely. She could see the lust in their eyes and it pissed her off and made her sick to her stomach. "Tell yo punk ass workers to stop looking at me like I'm a piece of meat. Ain't shit moving." She mugged them.

Makaroni looked over his shoulder at his crew. As soon as he did, they looked off. "Yo, let's go for a walk real fast." He waved to Cassidy and guided Montana toward the gangway of his trap. They entered into the duplex through the back side door. Within minutes, they were in the backroom, sitting on a couch. He pulled her on to his lap. "Talk to me lil' mama." Montana shook her head. "It's JaMichael. I think y'all about to have some major problems."

Makaroni felt his heart drop. "Why you say that?"

Montana exhaled loudly with her jaws poked out. She used this mechanism to calm herself down throughout the years. "Jahliya told me not to say nothing until she was sure they couldn't figure things out down there, but you're my brother. If I feel like some shit is going to affect you, I'ma let you know what's good right away. Damn what she talking about." She put her arm around his neck. His cologne was driving her crazy. She couldn't understand how her obsession had become so vast for him.

"Yeah, fuck what she talking about. Let bruh know what's good?" Makaroni maneuvered her so that she was facing him. He stroked her soft cheek to help her calm down. When she got riled up, she had a hard time thinking straight. "Come on, sis. Tell me what's up. Did I tell you how fine you looking right now?"

She smiled and lowered her head. "No. But you can."

"You killing shit. On everything, I ain't never seen nobody fuckin' wit' yo business. I'll admit that shit to anybody." He pulled her to him and kissed her lips.

Montana moaned into his mouth. "Damn, you fuckin' me up mentally." She ran her fingers through her hair. Her nipples were poking out against her dress. "Okay. Here we go. Jahliya said that Phoenix, and JaMichael are in a serious war over

Memphis. She doesn't know what the exact details are but it's costing JaMichael a lot of money. Money that doesn't belong to him, but some fool named Rubio Flores. Apparently, JaMichael has missed two serious payments to Rubio and he isn't happy about it. He has placed a substantial amount of interest on the first payment, and even more on the second. If JaMichael doesn't annihilate Phoenix, and fully take over Orange Mound, and White Haven." She caught herself. "I mean Black Haven, then he'll be forced to suffer the consequences from the Sinister Cartel. I've heard stories about how lethal and sick Rubio Flores can really be when it comes to his money."

Makaroni was confused. He frowned and imagined everything that JaMichael was going through. He felt nothing. "Fuck JaMichael. I mean, I get he our cousin and all that shit, but what the fuck he got going on got to do with me, or you for that matter? We out here eating. I been hitting his hand with everything that Rubio been asking for ever since the Rebirth been a part of the equation."

"Bruh, I get that shit, but that ain't how the cartel work. You see, JaMichael vouched for you. The only reason Rubio is fuckin' with you or Stevo is because of JaMichael. But when he looks to murder JaMichael, he gon' cut the branches off of his entire tree. You and Stevo are included. That's how that shit goes."

Makaroni felt heated. "So cuz them goofy ass niggas down there can't get they shit together, that's gon' effect what me and Stevo doing up here? Even though we getting money by the pile?"

Montana nodded. "Unfortunately, that's how it's gon' go."

Makaroni patted her on the side of the ass. She stood up, and so did he. "They got me fucked up, Montana. On some

real shit. That nigga JaMichael is his own man. I don't give a fuck what he doing as long as he keep them bricks coming." He punched his fist. "So, what you thinking I should do?"

"I think you should go down there and help him smash Phoenix. Once Phoenix is out of the way, then you ain't gotta worry about JaMichael collapsing. He'll be in control of Memphis, and everything should flow smoothly."

Makaroni wasn't trying to hear that. He didn't like the thought of being connected to JaMichael in the game. He felt like his cousin wasn't as smart as he was. Like he had been passed up from receiving the important genes from Taurus. "Montana, I don't wanna fuck wit' that nigga on that level. I don't know shit about Memphis. I didn't really like that ma'fucka when I was down there, and right now, I'm looking to conquer Milwaukee. Chicago coming next. We already laying the groundwork for that. If I gotta go down here and get involved in some beef that I don't have shit to do with, that's gon' stunt my growth up here. Me and Stevo got quotas we gotta make too. Everybody acting like they forgetting about that. That shit foul."

Montana lowered her head. "I wish I was a nigga. If I was, I'd go down there with you and wreck some stuff, but I'm not. I got a whole ass future that I'm trying to build for myself. I'm just worried about you. I wish you had never gotten involved with Rubio Flores. There is no winning when it comes to fuckin' with him." She walked up and slid her arms around his neck. "Mack, I love you so much, big bruh. If anything happen to you, it would literally crush me. I wouldn't know what to do. I would be lost."

He held her, growing angrier and angrier. Makaroni hated both JaMichael and Phoenix. He didn't care that they were related. He wished he could kill the both of them, and answer to Rubio Flores. He needed to find a way to cut JaMichael out of

the equation. "Alright, sis." He gripped her ass and rubbed all over it while he looked into her brown eyes. "I'm a holler at Stevo, and see what he wanna do, and we gon' go from there. If the homie wanna mount up, and crush Phoenix then that's what we gon' have to do. If he ain't feeling it, then I'm a have to figure things out on my own. It wouldn't be the first time."

Montana laid her head on his chest. "I believe in whatever you finna do. I know that out of all the men involved, that you are the most intelligent, and deadly." She stepped on her tippy toes, and sucked all over his lips. "I'ma let Jahliya know what's good. I'll holler at you later. Whatever you and Stevo decide, make sure that you and I connect again before we make our way down south. It's something about being with you up here that drives me insane."

Makaroni squeezed that ass again. "We good. I feel the same way."

* * *

Stevo turned up the gold bottle of Cristal and drank from it as if he were dying of thirst. He staggered across the room and planted his ass inside of the love seat. Beside it was a small mirror with residue from the Rebirth on it. He picked up his black AK and looked across the room to Makaroni. "Look dawg, I don't give a fuck about Phoenix, and I don't give a fuck about JaMichael's punk ass. That nigga almost got us killed. If Rubio wanna try and come at us because of how them goofy ass niggas fuckin' up, then we gotta go to war. It's as simple as that." He licked his index finger and sopped up some of the Rebirth residue from the mirror. He sucked it off of his finger.

Makaroni glared at him. He wanted to get at Stevo for fuckin' with the Rebirth, but he knew that the moment wouldn't have been the best time for either of them. So, he did the best he could to ignore it. "Look nigga, we signed up to

95

enter this game through JaMichael. That's all the Sinister Cartel see. If they gotta take him down, then they gotta take us down. That's just how that shit work."

"And it's like I said, if Rubio wanna come at us on that level then we finna go to war. In order for him to bring that bullshit, he gon' have to come through the Brew City. We don't know shit about Memphis, but we know about Milwaukee. The Brew City. He bring that bullshit up here and I'ma buss his brain. We don't stand a chance down there. But up here, we are good."

Makaroni saw that Stevo didn't get it. "Bruh, we ain't going to war with no block boys. We'll be getting at a million dollar organization. We only have a few thousand. That ma'fucka got millions. Not only that, but the only way that we eating is because of the Rebirth. If he cut that supply off, then he cut off our money. If we ain't got no money, we can't go to war with nobody. It's best that we go down there and annihilate Phoenix bitch ass. Smoke him, and then we can come back up here and get more money than we are doing right now.

Stevo's face was a murderous mug. He was caught between a rock and a hard place. JaMichael had them by the balls. "Bruh, if it was up to me, I would stank yo punk ass cousins and be done with both of them niggas. I don't give a fuck about them. I don't give a fuck about Memphis. Orange Mound, or Black Haven. I wish I could blow that whole city off of the map. Real talk."

"Yeah well, you can't. So, now what?" Makaroni sat back and puffed on his blunt of OG Kush.

"I ain't going down there. Fuck them. But I will send my hitta with you." He smiled and sat back on the couch with the AK still on his lap.

"Yo hitta? Who the fuck you talking about? We supposed to be in this shit together." Makaroni snapped.

"We is, but Milwaukee is my throne. Fuck Memphis. I got killas that need me here now. I ain't finna fuck up what I got going on for JaMichael. I'ma send DaBaby down there with you and two of my Stevo Gang lunatics. Anything you need done, they gone handle that shit right away. In addition to that, if you need me for anything give me a jingle and I'ma rotate down as well. But not until you seem like you can't handle shit. You got that?"

Makaroni stared at him. "Pussy nigga, you letting that Rebirth go to yo head or something? You finna leave me out on a limb?"

Stevo shook off his disrespect. "Aw, so you know that I'm fuckin' with the Rebirth?" He laughed. "Good. I was feening for a fix." He pulled two grams of Rebirth out of his pocket and dumped them out on the mirror. In minutes, he'd tooted four lines. He was high as a bird on steroids. "Look, Makaroni, fuck yo people. I ain't risking my foundation for them. My killas will be there on my behalf. While you're gone, I'ma run the city, and make sure that things get taken care of the right way because this is our home. Fuck playing Captain Save a Ho to Memphis." He closed his eyes.

Makaroni stood up with his fists balled. "This money shit is changing you. You think that just because you are seeing a few pennies that you're the man now, huh?"

DaBaby stepped into the living room and dropped two duffel bags of cash on the floor. He nodded what up to Makaroni. "Say Stevo, this three hundred thousand right here. One fifty in each bag. We gotta re-up. Product is shorter than a cricket's leg right now."

Stevo opened his eyes. His head was spinning. He could hear the music playing inside of his mind. A soothing hymn that brought him immense joy. "Nigga, I was just talking about you. You finna go down to Memphis right quick with

my right hand man. The reason I'm sending you is because I love that nigga right there. You are the closest person to me that I can find to watch his back. I need you to hit Memphis with that deadly thirst for blood type shit. Handle yo' business beside him and come on back. Time is money. So DaBaby, this is my nigga Makaroni. Makaroni, dis is DaBaby."

Makaroni nodded to him with an utter disdain in his heart for Stevo. "What's good, lil' homie?"

DaBaby smiled, and it quickly turned into an evil sneer. "When do we mob out? I can't wait to get my hands dirty?"

Makaroni didn't know what to say. He glared at Stevo again. "I see what it is, nigga. I'll be in touch." He left Stevo's trap with his temper boiling.

Chapter 11

Keaira paced back and forth inside of her bedroom. She held a .45 automatic in her hand. She stopped and aimed at a picture of Stevo that was on her dresser. She closed one eye and pretended to shoot him. "Bam! Den his ass will fall back, wishing he never came at me bogus." She said out loud to nobody in general.

It had been a few weeks since she'd asked Stacy to take care of Stevo for her. He'd agreed to handling him, but then had disappeared to Atlanta to take care of some street business that she'd not been privy to. That frustrated Keaira. She was extremely impatient. She wanted Stevo out of her life for good. Stacy promised to text her when he got back into town, and she couldn't wait. She aimed at the picture on her dresser again and imagined knocking Stevo's brains out of his head.

Kandace opened the door to her bedroom and stepped inside. She saw Keaira and froze. "Aw, my fault. I'm coming into the wrong room." She started to back out of it.

"Wait, wait, wait, lil' girl. Come here." Keaira called to her.

Kandace stopped and tried to open her eyes. She didn't feel like being scolded by her older sister. Sometimes, she felt that Keaira overdid it. She acted like she was more like her mother than a sister. That irritated Kandace. "What's up, Keaira?"

Keaira pulled her by the arm until she was standing in front of her. "Lil' girl, are you high?"

Kandace tried her best to open her eyes as wide as she could, but it was an impossible task. The Rebirth had a hold of her. She felt like she had gotten high off of the potent heroin for the first time. She couldn't control her senses no matter

how hard she tried to. "Girl, you bugging. I don't do no drugs." She closed her eyes and nodded for a full minute.

Keaira stood watching her with a hand over her mouth. "Oh my God. You off one of them pills, ain't you?"

Kandace waved her off. "I'm just tired. I need to lay down." She grabbed the knob to the door.

Keaira yanked her away from it. "Bitch, if you don't tell me what the fuck you done took, I'm finna beat yo ass senseless." She placed the .45 on top of the dresser and stepped into Kandace's face.

Kandace avoided eye contact with her. "Keaira, I don't feel like doing this with you. I ain't high off of nothing. I'm just tired. I thought this was my room, but clearly it's not. Now if you will excuse me." She grabbed the knob again.

Keaira backhanded her so hard that she busted her nose. Kandace flew backward, and fell to one knee, dizzy. She couldn't feel any pain because the Rebirth was coursing through her system. But she knew that she had been hit.

"Bitch, ain't nobody playing wit' you! You are sixteen years old! What the fuck did you take?" Keaira snapped.

Kandace stood up and wiped the blood from her nose. It dripped off of her fingers. "You are not my mother, Keaira. You got a whole ass son in the other room. Stand on him. I'm living my life. You need to live yours. Now, get the fuck out of my way."

Keaira was taken aback. "Excuse me? Did you just curse at me?"

Kandace held her silence for a moment. Blood dripped from her chin. "Please get out of my way."

"N'all, bitch. Since you wanna act grown, I'm finna beat yo lil' ass like you are grown." Keaira took her earrings out of her ear lobes. She cracked her knuckles. She didn't know what

had gotten into Kandace, but if she was dead set on doing all that, she could to beat it out of her.

Kandace was so high that she didn't understand what Keaira meant by what she'd said. She tried to nudge her sister out of the way as polite as she could. "Please move."

Keaira cocked back and punched her little sister right in the jaw like their mother was accustomed to doing her when Keaira was just little girl. Kandace flew backward into the dresser. The gun fell from atop it, and to the floor. "Bitch, you ain't finna be no dope fiend. I don't know who you kicking it with out there in those streets but that shit dead. You ain't finna see them no more. Now, tell me what you done took?" She screamed.

Kandace crawled around on her hands and knees. Her nose was pouring blood. She felt woozy. She inhaled and swallowed so much blood that it made her sick. "Why you always putting your hands on me?"

Keaira ignored her. She grabbed a handful of her hair and yanked her to her feet. "What did you take?"

"I ain't took nothing. Get off of me." She pushed Keaira as hard as she could.

Keaira grabbed a hold of her blouse and tore half of it from her frame. The sounds of the linen ripping resonated in the small room. Keaira flung her to the floor and straddled her. "Bitch, on my baby, if you don't tell me wat you took, I'm finna beat you to death." She slapped her across the face. "What did you take?"

Stevo opened the door and stuck his head into the room. He had been parked out front with the rest of his working girls. They were waiting for Kandace to come inside and grab a change of clothes. After fifteen minutes, Stevo had come to investigate what was taking so long. "Bitch, get the fuck up

off of her. What's wrong with you?" He hollered, grabbing a handful of Keaira's hair, and pulling her backward.

She kicked her feet wildly from the shock of being picked up by her hair. "Let me go, Stevo. Dis ain't got shit to do wit' yo punk ass." She beat at his hand that was balled into a fist. Her hair was tangled up into his fingers.

He let her go. "Bitch, that's my lil' baby. Don't no ma'fucka touch her but me."

Keaira gasped. "Yo lil' baby. Nigga, my sister is sixteen years old. You calling her yo' baby?" She swung out of pure anger and cracked him as hard as she could in the jaw. Her fist connected and sent him flying backward into the hallway. She saw Kandace struggling to get up.

"Aw, so bitch you been fucking wit' my baby daddy behind my back? Really!" She ran at her sister with the intent to beat her senseless. Not only was she doing drugs, but she was messing around with grown men. Or at least one grown man. Keaira felt betrayed and pissed off.

Kandace scooted backward on the floor after grabbing the gun off of it. Her face was full of blood. "Don't come near me. I'm tired of you always hitting me."

Keaira froze in her tracks. She refused to believe that Kandace would shoot her, or that she even knew how to handle a gun. There was no way that she was going to allow for her to escape the ass whooping that she had coming. She threw caution to the wind and got ready to pounce on her.

Boom!

Keaira jumped backward. She felt the stinging pain in her stomach. She looked down, and saw the blood pouring out of her. She covered the massive hole with her right hand. Blood leaked through her fingers. Steven began to cry loudly from the other room as if he could feel the pain that his mother had been subjected to. Keaira staggered backwards.

102

Kandace made her way to her feet. "I told you I'm tired of you putting your hands on me."

Stevo stepped into the room with his eyes wide. He watched Keaira fall into the dresser. Blood leaked from her stomach to the carpet beneath her feet. "Baby, you popped this bitch?" He grew excited. He slid beside Kandace and kissed her forehead. "She don't wanna see us together anyway. She always been jealous of you. But can't nobody stop us from doing our thing. It's me and you for the rest of our life. Pop that bitch again. Fuck her." He urged. He knew how the Rebirth fucked with a person's mind. It brought the lunatic out of you when you least expected it too. Stevo saw a way for him to get rid of Keaira for good. He didn't want nothing else to do with her.

Keaira fell to her back. She struggled to get up, driven by anger and betrayal. She made it to her feet. The bullet spinning inside of her stomach felt like a hundred flaming swords to the gut. "Don't listen to him, Kandace. That nigga is the devil."

Kandace felt a strong trace of remorse. The blood lost coming from her nose caused a nice amount of the Rebirth to leave from her system. She came back to reality as more blood dropped from her chin. "I'm sorry, Keaira. I didn't mean to. You was finna attack me and I panicked."

Keaira hunched over, holding her stomach. "It's okay. Just give me the gun."

Stevo pulled Kandace backward. He got behind her. "N'all, baby. We ain't gon' do that. Dis is me and you now. You're my baby girl. Fuck this bitch. She done hated you ever since you came out of your mama. We can never be together if she is alive. It's either you choose me, or you choose her. And you know what I can bring to the table." He pulled out a twenty thousand dollar knot. Put it under her nose. Next, was

an ounce of the Rebirth. "You smoke this bitch and you can party all night. If you don't, then bitch you dead to me."

Kandace shivered. She looked out at her sister. She wanted to save her. She hadn't meant to shoot her. But now it was too late. She thought. "Please don't make me do this, Stevo."

"Baby, you can do whatever you want. I want you, but I don't need you. I got a truck full of women downstairs. I know Sasha will love to be my bottom bitch. She can't wait to re-place you as my Queen. Just as we getting our money right, too." He release his hold on her. "Fuck you, Kandace. You are dead to me." He walked out of the room and got ready to close the door.

"Stevo, wait!" Kandace called.

Keaira saw her moment. She jumped to grab the gun away from Kandace. Her brain told her that she was stronger than her body actually was. Before she could grab the gun, her legs gave out. She smacked the pistol and it went off.

Boom!

Keaira felt the round punch through the middle of her nose. It shot a direct path through her nasal passage and knocked a huge chunk of her brain out the back of her head. She was dead before she hit the ground.

Kandace dropped the gun and began to scream. A puddle formed around Keaira's head. She dropped to the floor and tried to help her sister. It was of no use. She was gone.

Stevo stepped back into the room with a big smile on his face. "Holy shit!" He knelt beside Kandace. "Baby, shut up. Stop all that ma'fuckin' screaming before the other hoes hear you."

Kandace covered her mouth. Only slight traces of the Re-birth were in her system. She moved her hand. "I didn't do it, she did. I swear to God I didn't kill my sister." Her eyes crossed. She fainted from the sheer shock of it all.

Stevo stood up. He poked at Keaira with his Balenciaga. He expected her to move. She didn't. He checked her pulse. Once again, there was nothing. He smiled. "Bitch gone." He backed up. He could hear Steven crying in the other room. He looked down on the sisters again. One was dead, the other knocked out cold. He jogged from the room.

He opened Steven's door. The little boy stood up in his bed crying his heart out. When he saw Stevo, he reached out for him. Stevo backed up. He felt his heart turning cold. He pulled out a bag of the Rebirth and tooted a sixteenth of it. The high took over him suddenly. He replaced the remainder of the drug. "I'm tired of child support. Tired of all of this shit." He picked Steven up, and slammed him to the bed. He grabbed a pillow and placed it over his face. He applied as much pressure as he could while Steven's legs kicked wildly. "Die muthafucka. I'm done with her. I'm done with you." He smothered him for five minutes straight. When he backed away from his son, he was lifeless. He yanked him up by the arm and brought him into the room with Keaira and Kandace. His next move was to call DaBaby.

***

Four hours later, DaBaby had chopped Keaira to pieces, along with Steven. He was under the impression that somebody had tried to attack Stevo's family and had succeeded. His orders were to get rid of the bodies and meet Stevo back at their headquarters. He didn't ask questions. He simply followed Stevo's orders. He was the one feeding him and making sure that he was able to put food on his family's table. That was all that mattered.

He threw pieces of Keaira into the river one by one until she was done. Next, came Steven. After he had successfully

completed his task, he texted Stevo to let him know that he was on his way.

Stevo rubbed alcohol onto a crying Kandace's inner forearm. He found a hefty vein and slid the needle of the syringe into it. "Just chill, baby. Daddy got you. We gone take all of that pain away. I got you." He eased down on the feeder and pumped a strong dose of the Rebirth into Kandace's system.

Kandace's eyes rolled into the back of her head. She felt the drug shooting all over her. Her tears stopped. A broad smile came across her face. Her eye lids closed tightly. "Keaira." She whispered, then she was out and mentally into another world.

Stevo eased her back on the couch, and covered her lower naked half with a blanket. He sat beside her, and rubbed her angelic face. "It's all good baby. You did good. You did real good." He took a sip from his gold bottle of Ace of Spades. "On to the next chapter," He said out loud.

Chapter 12

Makaroni tossed his suitcase into the backseat of his truck. He closed the door, and rested his back against it. "Man, I don't feel like going down here and fucking with them. Everything is starting to go right in our city. Fuck theirs."

Montana stepped into his face, then backed up. She had to remember that they were standing outside where everybody could see them. She could tell that Makaroni was angry. She needed to calm him down before he left for Memphis later that night. He needed to have a clear head. She didn't know for sure what he would be walking into.

"Big bruh, can you and I please spend a few hours together before you hit the road. Please? I ain't gon be able to follow you down there for a few days I just wanna make sure that we got our minds right before we part."

The block was alive and busy. Nearly every porch had a person on it. All eyes seemed to be on Makaroni and Montana. It didn't help that Montana was wearing a skintight red and blue Fendi dress that fit her like a second skin. She was without a bra because the dress didn't call for one. Her nipples poked through the fabric.

"The sooner I get on the road, the sooner I can get down there and back. I ain't trying to be stuck in Memphis forever."

Montana stepped closer. She was starting to not care about the onlookers. "Listen to me, Makaroni. I know how you are when you are angry. You don't make the wisest decisions. You are going into a situation where you have to be a thinker in order to conquer it. If you are angry, there is no way that you will be able to outthink the other players in the Game. In this case, your brain is the only thing that will keep us alive. It won't be how many guns you take down there, or how many

killas. That's for damn sure. It'll be your mind. Do you understand me?"

Makaroni looked her over from his Chanel sunglasses. He couldn't help but to see the logic in what Montana was spitting at him. She made a lot of sense. Sometimes, he forgot about the fact that he was born only a few minutes apart from her. "You know what, Montana? You're right. I'm so ma'fuckin' mad right now that I can't think straight. All I keep thinking about is the fact that I gotta go down here to this city and fix some shit that two grown ass men screwed up. That's irritating. I shouldn't have to do that. I should be able to stay right here in the Brew City and get out foundation together. I gotta leave this nigga Stevo in control of all of my shit. That ain't sitting right with me."

"I know it ain't. But you gotta do what you gotta do. You are the most powerful piece. That's why they need you to fix all of this shit that they screwed up. Its common sense." She looked to her right and saw a group of dudes ogling her. They disgusted her. She hated them even though she didn't know them. The only man she cared about was Makaroni. She no longer felt guilty for feeling that way either. Her brother was her world. Outside of her mother, he was the only person that she cared about in life. "Hey, look at me. Can we please just chill tonight? Can we just sit back and watch a movie together before you get on the road? Please?"

Makaroni lowered his head. He picked it up, and exhaled loudly praying that it would help him to calm down, but it had very little effect on his overall mood. "I should be getting on this road, Montana. I still gotta stop by Stevo trap and pick up DaBaby."

Montana poked out her bottom lip. She gave him the sad puppy dog look. She grabbed his left hand. "Come on now, Mack. I need you. Life is way too short. We never know when

we will breathe our last breath. All I'm asking for is a night where we kick back like we used to do when we were kids. Is that too much to ask?"

He looked her up and down. She turned into a little girl of eight years old right before his eyes. He saw the pigtails. The barrettes in her hair. Her holding her favorite Barbie Doll. He imagined it all. Then, she grew back up to the age of twenty-one. He snapped out of his zone. "Yeah, sis. That's cool. I'll just hit the road the first thing in the morning."

Montana rushed him and hugged him as tight as she could. "That's why I love you so damn much. That's why you are my heart." She grabbed his hands and led him toward the house.

***

"Awright. Awright. Awright. Everybody settle down." Stevo stepped to the front of the rented ballroom with a gold bottle of Ace of Spades in one hand, and Sasha's hand in his other. He made sure that she looked flawless. She was dressed in an Eves St. Laurent red and black form fitting evening gown that left her cleavage on display, with Balenciaga heels. Her short curly hair was full of sheen. He led her to a seat beside his own. He remained standing. The ballroom was full of his killas. They were young goons that he'd recruited from the slums of Chicago, and Milwaukee. He'd picked only the starving. He chose project kids that had nothing to lose and everything to gain. Soldiers that he could brain wash into honoring him as a young God. They looked up to him with fear and admiration.

"Everybody take a seat. I got something to say." He waited until the room was seated. Chairs scratched across the floor. People murmured to each other before they all sat down and grew quiet. Only then, did he speak with DaBaby standing behind him on security. "Now that we have taken over Highland,

and the London Square Apartments, it's time that we get money in a major way. I'm ready to see all of my niggas riding foreign. I wanna see you hustlers living in condos, and buying houses out there with the rich white folk. You should never have to lay your head in the hood. We done did that long enough. This is a new day. A day where we go from being low lives to living the high life. He searched the faces of each man. He wanted to make sure that he had their undivided attention. "Now that y'all run under me, it's my job to make sure that you are financially secure, and stable within this Game. Everything starts with me. I am the head. You are the body."

DaBaby left the room and came back with a long suitcase. He opened it up and pulled out an AR .33 assault rifle with a HD scope on top of it.

"This is a military issued AR .33. It is one of the most accurate assault rifles in the business, and because of me, we just got a hundred of them from my connect out in Vegas. You see while Stevo may be the head but when it comes to this killa shit, I am the shoulders. The head needs to shoulders to balance the body. That's where I come in at."

Stevo snickered. "Yeah, that's real. In addition to these new weapons, we are looking to expand our operations a lil' bit. We got a new plug coming out of Vegas that's gone hit us with some of the pinkest Girl in America. This coke gone knock our customers' socks off. Only the best. We getting it at ninety percent, and we getting rid of it the same way. The goal is to snatch up as many clients has we can. After we hook the city, then we can start stepping on our product just a little bit, but not until then. Each one of you will play a special part in this rise from the gutters. We are a family here. When you look to your left, you should hope to see that your brother is successful. The same goes for the right. As long as they are, you should be doing just as well in the middle. If all of us are

flourishing there is no way that we can fail." He held up his bottle of Champagne. "To conquering the slums, and making the mafuckas that doubted us kiss our ass."

The room broke into fits of cheering. They laughed. They clapped hands. They believed in the future that Stevo was painting for them. Stevo smiled as he looked around. In his mind, each man was expendable. He didn't give two fucks about either of them. He promised to find a way to use each man to make him richer. That's what the game was all about. It was manipulating the mentally weak, and using them to strengthen your own self. Stevo knew this, and he took it to the heart. As long as they thought that he had their best interests at heart, they would do anything for him. He had them right where he needed them to be.

"Awright, bruh. Now release the hoes." Stevo stood up, and summoned the fifty strippers that he had hired for the night to take care of his men. Strippers were some of his best customers when it came to getting rid of the Rebirth. He promised the girls an ounce of the Rebirth to split, plus fifty percent of their tips, and they were all in. He sat back and marveled at what he created. He pulled Sasha on to his lap. "You see this, baby girl? Huh? Do you see how these niggas honor me?"

Sasha was high, and amazed. She had to admit that she was dealing with a boss. "Yeah, daddy, I see."

"That's why you gotta play yo role to the tee. If you wanna live good and be a boss bitch, you gon' have to jockey for position. Ain't shit free in this world. You think a mafucka care because how fine you look? Huh? Matter fact, get off of my lap." He flipped her off of him and to the floor. "Get yo ass up and go make that money with the rest of them hoes and bring back every penny to me. You hear me?"

Sasha got to her feet. "Yes, daddy." She felt terrible. She scurried off to find a male to give a lap dance too.

Stevo kicked this feet up on the table. DaBaby stood behind him ready to wet something. Stevo drank from his bottle of Champagne feeling like a boss. Everybody that had ever called him a bum was the reason that he was acting like he was acting. He didn't give a care about nothing, and nobody. Being broke for so long had turned him into a monster.

***

Montana stood at the foot of the hotel bed dressed in a pair of white lace boy shorts, and a matching Victoria Secret bra. She climbed across the bed and pulled the covers back, situating herself with her back to Makaroni. She made sure that her ass was in his lap. She pulled his right hand over her. She could feel his muscular chest on her back. "So, what movie are we about to watch?"

Makaroni started it. "Queen and Slim. I wanna see what this movie is all about."

"Yeah, me too." She laid her head on his chest as best she could. She could feel the length of his piece resting along her ass crack. "Makaroni before we watch this movie, can we talk for a second?"

He stopped the movie by use of the remote. "What's good?"

"I'm worried about you going down there to Memphis. I just got a terrible feeling in my gut about this whole thing." She admitted.

"To be honest with you, I do too. I mean I ain't scared or no shit like that, but I am a lil' worried about how things are going to turn out. I been having bad dreams about it and all of that shit."

Montana turned around so that she was facing him. She grabbed his big hand, and clasped her fingers with his. "What

happens in your dreams?" She wanted to know. She was hoping that he wasn't seeing death or anything like that.

"I can't really say for certain, but shit just go awry. I really don't wanna talk about it because I really don't have a choice. I gotta go down there, or Rubio and his cartel gon' come up here to get at me. Its smarter for me to get ahead of everything than behind it."

Montana rubbed the side of his face. "I hate that you gotta go through this, bruh. Life shouldn't have to be so hard. I wish that daddy never walked out on our family. Maybe me and you wouldn't be so screwed up. Well, me anyway. I'm so afraid of men that I'm falling in love with you and I ain't even trying to fight it. You're the only man that has ever really loved me with all of your heart. That means more to me than you will ever know. I wish I could protect you. I swear to God I would to the best of my ability." She continued to rub his face softly.

Makaroni gazed into her eyes. He hated himself for feeling so weak when he looked into them. He felt like he could see her broken soul. He saw the reflection of his own broken self. That made him love her even harder. "Montana, I love the fuck out of you. I mean I know that sooner or later we gotta stop being scared and take chances on other people outside of ourselves because we can't keep doing this." He felt so lost. He took a deep breath, and blew it out of his nostrils. "Man, sis in this moment, I love you more than anybody on earth. That same in love feeling that you are feeling, I feel too. That's why we gotta break this shit up. It's too dangerous. Anywhere we go beyond this is dangerous."

Montana kissed his lips. "I don't care. We are all that we have. This world is full of snakes and rats. We can't trust it. You see how daddy did mama. You see how destructive their relationship was. She did some things and so did he. I don't wanna go through that. We shouldn't have too. I love you and

you are all I need. I wish that could be okay. I wish you didn't have to go down there and we could run away forever. I mean that."

Makaroni rested his forehead against hers. He kissed her lips once, then twice ever so softly. "I wish I didn't have to either, but what has to be done must be done."

I guess you're right. I trust you, though." She kissed his lips again.

"What do you mean?"

"I trust you to go down there and to master that situation. There is nobody else that can do it other than you. But before you do, I just want you to hold me all night through. Hold me tight, and don't let me go. Please." She snuggled up to him.

Makaroni hugged her into his arms, and placed his nose against the back of her head. Her ass seemed to fit perfectly in his lap. He felt himself getting hard but ignored it. He was sure that Montana didn't want this night to be about sex. It was more of an emotional thing for her. He wanted to meet her where she needed him most. He kissed her scalp. "I love you, lil' baby. I'ma go down here and handle this business for us. I promise you that."

Montana smiled, scooted back on him and closed her eyes. "I know you will. While you're gone, I'ma make sure Stevo is keeping everything on the up and up. You got my word. Now hold me. I need you right now."

"You know I got you." He held her as firm as he could. He felt complete, yet determined.

Chapter 13

Makaroni pulled into Memphis the next day just as the sun was going down. His Eddie Bauer truck vibrated as it rolled down the cracked road of the highway leading into the city. He felt a sudden case of butterflies as he passed the sign welcoming him into the city of Memphis, Tennessee. He could only remember how it had all kicked off when both he and Stevo had gotten there the last time.

DaBaby adjusted his twin Glocks on his waist. He took one and placed it on his lap. Then, he pulled his black tee shirt back over his weapon. "So, dis Memphis, huh? Mafuckas be making it seem like dis city bout that action, so I just wanna make sho' that I'm prepared for whatever finna pop off down here. I heard them country niggas be some of the craziest. They say they got us Chicago niggas beat."

Roscoe, a heavyset, dark skinned killa with a bald head, grunted. "Yeah, we'll see about that." He held an assault rifle on his lap with it locked and ready to blow. DaBaby had personally picked him to tag along for the Memphis run. They were old running buddies back in Chicago. Between the two, they had a total of thirty bodies under their belt. Like DaBaby, Roscoe was also from the Village, a deadly housing project located in the slums of Chicago, Illinois. There, it was kill or be killed.

DaBaby looked back at him, and nodded. "Nigga, you already know what it is. If anything look funny, you blow that shit down like the wolf in the Three Little Pigs."

"You already know that, kinfolk." Roscoe scanned the streets as Makaroni got off of the highway. His trigger finger was itching.

Makaroni texted Jahliya that he was in town, and that he would be meeting her at Al's Bowling alley just outside of

White Haven. "Say DaBaby, I'm finna meet up with my cousin right now to find out what's really good? We probably gon' sit back and have lunch. I need for y'all to chill and stay on security. Awright?"

DaBaby nodded. "This ain't our first rodeo, homeboy. We know we ain't here to mingle. Shid, we more interested in when the killing gon' start more than anythang else." He looked back at Roscoe once again. Roscoe was scanned as if he was expecting a shooter to jump out at them in any second.

"Cool then. I just wanna see what's up cause I ain't tryna be down here for a long ass time."

"Say no more, homie. Do whatever you gotta do."

Makaroni drove with his phone on his lap. He came through the lights, and made a left. The road took him directly to Al's big parking lot. Before he even pulled inside of it, he saw Jahliya's dark purple Range Rover. He pulled up alongside of it. He could hear the sounds of Summer Walker's album coming out of her speakers. He parked, and jumped out of his truck.

Jahliya stepped out of her Range Rover dressed in Prada from head to toe. Her long curly hair was pulled back by a black and purple Prada hair clip. She had on a black and purple Prada skirt, over a matching top. The skirt conformed to her backside. She slipped into Makaroni's arms and hugged him tightly. "Hey, lil' cuz. It's good to see that you made it here safe and sound."

Makaroni kissed both of her cheeks. "I'm on business. We need to sit down, and have dinner so you can tell me what I'm walking into."

"That's cool. Come on, we can snatch up something to eat at Al's. They got these double cheeseburgers in here that taste like heaven." She saw DaBaby moving in the passenger's seat.

She slipped her hand into purse, and around her .40 Glock. "Cuz, you brought somebody down here wit' you?"

Makaroni saw where she was looking. "Yeah, two of my hittas. I wanted to bring a few lil' niggas that ain't got no attachment to none of this. Fresh eyes, so that's what I did."

"Yeah, well is any one of those dudes that nigga that you brought down here the last time you came? What was his name Steven, Kevo, or somethin' like that?"

"Nall, and his name was Stevo. He back in Milwaukee making sure that everything run smoothly."

"Oh, really? And whose idea was that? Yours or his?"

"Both of ours."

Jahliya grunted. "Sounds like to me that he on some fuck you type shit. Ain't no real friend finna let you come all the way down here to Memphis so you can go to war on your own. All it sounds like he care about is y'all money. Not knowing that if things don't go right down here, it ain't gone be no money for any of us to look after. It's gone be all about bullets and bloodshed. Come on, let's go in here and order. We got a lot of catching up to do."

***

Sasha stepped out of the shower and wrapped her hair in a pink terry cloth towel. She took the second big towel and wrapped it around her body. She started to tuck in the sides when Kandace knocked on the bathroom door.

"Who is it?" Sasha asked.

"Me girl, I gotta pee." Kandace informed her.

Sasha unlocked the door and stepped to the side. She closed it back and locked it. "Hey."

Kandace sat right on the toilet and released her bladder. She had been holding her piss for thirty minutes after waking up. The whole time she'd been praying that Sasha was going

to come out of the bathroom until finally she couldn't hold it anymore. She watched Sasha getting dressed and had to nod her head at how gorgeous her body actually was. "Girl, why you getting all dressed up for?"

Sasha slid the Fendi dress over her head. She smoothed it against her soft skin and fluffed her hair over her slender shoulders. "Stevo told me to get ready so that I could come to him. He said I earned it." She smiled and went back to fixing herself up in the mirror.

Kandace finished her business. She washed her hands. After she finished, she stood with her arms crossed, mugging Sasha with pure jealousy. "What the hell does that mean? You're going to him?"

"It means that I'm finally finna see what that thing like between his thighs. I've been yearning for it. He told me that he would never fuck me until I earned it. Well, now I have. I can't wait." She was giddy. She opened a container of Sephora make up and went to work turning herself into a beauty queen.

"What did you do that was so spectacular?" Kandace asked dryly.

She was thinking that surely it couldn't have been more than taking part in her own sister's death. She felt angry and disgusted. She wondered what Stevo could've possibly been thinking. Maybe he thought that she was still ill because of what had happened to Keaira. She reasoned with herself. She was thinking that she should let him know that she was feeling somewhat better. That she was ready to lay down for him. Then, he wouldn't need Sasha to lay down in her place.

Sasha shrugged. "I don't really know why he feel like I earned him. I mean, I made a lot of money from giving lap dances the other day when he took me to that ballroom. That's really the only thing that I could think of. But either way, I'm

happy that it's my turn. I need me some of him." She put on her fake eyelashes.

Kandace stepped closer to her. "Bitch, you already know that ain't nobody supposed to be sleeping with him but me. I been feeling a bit under the weather." She lied. "But I'm good now. You can take yo ass back in your room and lay it down. I'll handle Stevo."

Sasha smacked her lips. "Girl, if you don't get yo funky breath ass out my face and stay in yo lane, we gon' have a problem." She rolled her eyes and went back to making sure that her right eyelash was on perfect, before she moved to the left one.

Kandace felt herself shaking. She rested her hand on the sink and spoke to Sasha's reflection in the mirror. "Sasha, I'm gon' give you a final warning. Do not take your yellow ass in that room and do anything with Stevo. If you don't listen to me, I can't be held responsible for what I do to you."

Sasha scoffed. "Bitch, the first thing you should do when you get up in the morning is brush your fuckin' teeth. Especially, if you are planning on talking to anybody. Secondly, if you really knew me you would know that I'm a Latina, baby. I don't scare easily. I'm from the south side, bitch. My life was horrible. I ain't run away for nothing." She turned to face Kandace. "Now, I like Stevo. He a grown ass man and I like grown dick. He fine. He's a killa. That's up my alley. That's my daddy. If you got a problem with it, then you do what you gotta do. I'm finna go fuck him in the worst way." She snickered. "You already knew I was badder than you. That's yo fault for letting me be a part of this stable. Can't no black bitch fuck with us Spanish hoes."

Kandace smiled. She felt like a damn fool. She felt herself shaking. She was so angry that she felt like hauling off and punching Sasha. "Awright, Sasha. Well, you gon' in there and

you have fun. I wish you the best." She grabbed her tooth-brush, and Crest toothpaste. She left the bathroom with devi-ous thoughts going through her mind. She yearned for the Re-birth.

Stevo was coming out of the kitchen in just his boxers and black beater. "Hey baby. Give daddy a hug."

Kandace bumped him and kept it moving. "Hug that bitch in the bathroom. I'm finna brush my teeth."

Stevo felt like grabbing her by the hair, and beating her ass, but he laughed it off. "Yeah aiight, shorty. Yo Sasha, hurry yo ass up Mami." He had plans on tearing the Puerto Rican girl up.

***

"Now, JaMichael should have an entire strategy already in place to go at Phoenix. I don't know what it is for sure, but I do know that he is the key in preventing all of us from going to war with Rubio Flores. Y'all get rid of him, and we'll all be able to live to see another day. Our money increases, and we'll be able to grow, and expand our family's businesses." Jahliya picked up her lemonade and sipped out of it.

Makaroni ran his right hand over his waves. "I can't be-lieve that Memphis is that important in everything. What the fuck is so good about this city?" Makaroni really didn't get it. From as far as he saw, the city seemed a bit ran down to him. He looked like it was slowly dying. He got an eerie feeling just from being in it.

"Memphis is a dumping post for the cartel. They dump off large quantities of narcotics, and JaMichael and Phoenix dis-tribute it all over the United States. The dumping post used to be Phoenix, Arizona but the Feds shut that down after El Chapo's son had that major shootout down in Mexico when the authorities tried to apprehend him. Many innocent lives were lost that day, and now they are on him. He is rumored to

be living there so they are all over it. Anyway, Memphis belongs to the Side Sinister Cartel. They are the newest, and most strong cartel operating out of Mexico right now. Both Phoenix and JaMichael have a certain rapport with Rubio Flores. He's gotten both of them filthy rich. Now, he's looking to only use one of them because his operations for a reason that I haven't been told is expanding to other forms of narcotics. Out of love, and honor for our father, Taurus, Rubio Flores is willing to allow our bloodline to be in control of the Rebirth. But he will only allow for one man to be his underboss when it comes to the Rebirth. Both JaMichael, and Phoenix want to be that man. They both cannot be. In addition to that, when it comes to the Cartel world, after a boss is stripped of his position, he is killed in a deadly fashion. Whichever one of these men that Rubio Flores chooses to head the Rebirth, the other will be killed in cold blood. That's how it goes. That's how it's going to be. That's why each man is looking to get rid of the other before Rubio can choose on his own. Rumor has it that he will be making this decision on his son's birthday."

"When is that?"

"March tenth. We have two weeks to get rid of Phoenix or we stand a fifty percent chance of losing JaMichael, and myself."

"Wait, how would we lose you?" Makaroni was confused.

"I got my hand in everything that JaMichael has his hand in. It's because of the Rebirth that I've been able to open up three strip clubs, and four other businesses. I'm into real estate. We're acquiring property weekly. All of these things are sanctioned by the Sinister Cartel. When you enter into this Game, Makaroni, there is nothing you can do without getting their approval first. You must kick back everything to Rubio Flores and his henchmen. If you don't, and he finds out about

it, you're going to be in big trouble." Jahliya ate a French fry. "You like your cheeseburger?"

Makaroni sat back away from his food. He didn't know how she could eat anything when there was so much at stake. "Damn, Jahliya, I ain't gon' even lie, if I knew that the Game was this fucked up, I would have taken my ass to school and got an education. It seem like no matter what you do you are destined to fail."

She nodded. "Everybody think that when they see us rolling our trucks and dressing in designer that we are living the life. It may sound fucked up, but the poorest of people are the free ones."

"I believe that now." Makaroni shook his head. "Well, since Montana working under you, and you are involved with Rubio Flores by way of JaMichael, I'm choosing to fuck wit' JaMichael to get rid of Phoenix. Hit him up and tell him what's good. We need to crush Phoenix immediately."

Jahliya smiled. "I agree."

Chapter 14

Sasha stepped into Stevo's bedroom and closed the door behind herself. The shades were drawn. Stevo had a red-light bulb screwed into both lamps that sat on stands on each side of the bed. She felt nervous. She blew air out of her lungs with her jaws puffed out. She slowly stepped to the foot of the bed, and then around until she was standing in front of him.

Stevo grabbed her by the waist and pulled her closer to him. "What's the matter, baby girl? You nervous?" It was like he could smell the fear coming off of her. It coupled with her perfume that drew him into her.

Sasha shook her head. "Nah, I'm not scared. I just wanna be perfect for you, daddy. Am I?" She batted her fake eyelashes and puckered her lips.

Stevo laughed. Then, he grew serious. "Ain't no such thang as a perfect woman. All you bitches got imperfections. The reason why I chose you is because I see something special inside of you. You have the ability to be a strong part of the empire that I am building. It ain't got shit to do with you being perfect. You are only perfect when I say you are. That's when you prove yourself to me. You understand me?"

Sasha nodded. "Yes, Daddy."

"Awright, but in this moment it ain't about perfection. It's about me seeing what you got between these lil' thighs. I wanna know how fresh this shit is before I put it out on the market. If it's too fresh, you gon' belong solely to me. Would you have a problem with that?"

"N—" She began.

"Bitch, I wouldn't care if you did." Stevo interrupted her. He gripped her ass and squeezed her soft cheeks. The meat sunk in between the gaps of his fingers. "Damn, yo lil' ass thick."

Hearing her confirm it made Stevo's dick harder. H remembered how girls treated him back in high school. How they used to shit on him because he couldn't dress as fresh as the rest of the kids in school. He remembered running across flawless dime pieces like Sasha when he was her age. Females like her would never give him the time of the day. But now, he was in control. Now, he was ready to fuck and rule as many of them as he could. He would start with Sasha. She could've quite possibly been the finest female he had ever seen in his entire life. She drove him crazy, but he would make her pay for the sins of all of the girls that came before her, that looked like her.

Stevo held her right thigh in his forearm while he kissed all over her fresh pussy. His tongue invaded her crevice. He slurped and licked up and down her slit. He swallowed her juices. He stuck his tongue as far into as it could go. When it was deep, he brushed his nose from side to side against her clitoris. His face was coated with her juices. He sucked her clit hard.

Sasha's back was arched so much that she looked like a bridge. She inhaled and screamed as loud as she could. Stevo flicked her clit over and over until she started to squirt in his face.

He nearly came in his pants. He licked her pee hole as the cum flew out of it. He sucked and swallowed. Then, he got up, and got undressed. "Huh. Handle this."

Sasha was weak. She came to her knees and crawled across the bed. She was still shaking when she took him into her hand and stroked him for ten seconds. She sucked the head into her mouth and went to work. Her head game was basic. She needed work, but she was young. Stevo understood that. He grabbed a handful of her hair, and slow stroked her until she gagged around him.

"That's okay, baby. Suck daddy. You wanna be my bottom bitch? Huh? Then, taste me."

Sasha closed her eyes and began to breathe through her nose. Every time the soft head of his dick would touch her tonsils, she'd gag. Spit would emit from her throat. She tried to pull back, but he forced her to take more of him.

"Bottom bitches gotta work. That's just that." He pulled out of her mouth, stroking himself. He jerked. His eyes were on her dime face and the brown areolas of her breasts. He came, shooting jets all over her face. He grabbed her and rubbed his piece all over her face.

Sasha felt the hot cream, and something about it excited her. She didn't think that she could make a boss like Stevo cum. But now that he did, she felt special. She felt powerful. She accepted his seed all over her face as a badge of honor.

Stevo pumped his ten inch monster. It was erect with thick veins going through it. It didn't lose an inch of its hardness after cuming. He fed his pipe to Sasha. "Just suck on the head, baby."

Sasha followed his commands. "Yes, Daddy." She licked all over him and sucked the head like a pro. Stevo saw right away that she didn't have a sucking problem, she had a length problem. She did a good job at shielding her teeth. Her lip play was excellent. She knew just when to add her tongue, and even a bit of teeth just slightly. He felt like cuming again in a matter of seconds. He pushed her off of him. The next time he came, he wanted it to be inside of her coochie.

Sasha laid on her back. She rubbed her pussy. Her face was flushed. "Now what, Daddy?"

Stevo climbed between her thighs. He rubbed her gash. Her pussy lips were puffy, and engorged from her excitement. He took his dick head, and placed it on her entrance. He cocked back, and slammed it home.

126

"Uhhhh! Shit!" Sasha went into convulsions. She couldn't help cuming from first contact with his penis.

Stevo stroked her like a savage animal. He imagined all of the females in his school that had ever crapped on him. He fucked her harder and harder, long stroking her insides.

Sasha squeezed her eyes closed. She dug her nails into his side. He had her so full that she felt like she was losing her breath. She tried to scoot from under him just a bit to relieve some of the penetration but it was of no use. Stevo pushed her knees to her chest and fucked her like he hated her. "You mine. You mine Sasha. Yo. Fine. Ass. Belong. To. Me!"

Tap. Tap. Tap. Tap. Went the headboard after more stroking. He growled, and slammed into her as hard as he could.

Sasha squirted all over him twice in a row. She screamed. She scratched at the sheets. She pulled the sheets off of the bed, and bit on it. Tears leaked out of her eyes, and ran down her cheeks. Stevo paid no attention to this. He kept fucking her tight pussy.

Kandace took her ear off of the door. She punched her hand in anger. She ran down to the linen closet and retrieved the .9 millimeter that she knew Stevo kept there. Tears ran down her beautiful face. She couldn't believe that he would do this to her. After everything that they had been through. She thought that she was his little baby. She never imagined that he would choose Sasha over her. It wasn't fair. She kept telling herself. It just wasn't fair. She got up the nerve to kill Sasha. She felt that if she killed her that Stevo would never chose another female over her ever again. He would see that she truly loved him. That she was willing to do anything for him again. "Dis bitch finna die!" She hollered.

Stevo flipped Sasha over to her stomach and laid on her back. He sunk his long dick into her hot pocket slowly. Her sex lips spread wider and wider to accept him. He was

pumping like a bull in heat. He was hopping up and down on the cushions of her golden colored ass cheeks.

"Daddy. Daddy. Awww. Shit. Shit. Shit. Daddy. It's too much! It's too much. Unnnn!" She collapsed from cuming so hard. Stevo was putting down that grown dick in a major way. He wanted to lock Sasha down. He wanted to make sure that he would never have to worry about her going anywhere.

"You. Earned. This. Dick. Baby. Girl. Fuck. You. Earned. It." He humped faster and faster. Sweat dripped off of his face. He was oblivious to the fact that Sasha had fainted. He pulled her up to her knees and kept pounding while her face drug up and down the sheets. Twenty pumps later, he was cuming deep in her womb. He pulled out and tossed her to her stomach.

Sasha woke up when she landed on her chest. Hot drips of Stevo's seed landed on her ass cheeks, and lower back. She felt her pussy hole pounding from his savagery. She prayed that it was over. She wasn't ready for him. She was okay with admitting that.

Stevo flipped her over. "You good, baby?" His dick ran up and down her slit.

She nodded, breathing hard. "I can't handle you. I ain't in your league. You are a grown ass man." She was out of breath.

Stevo laughed. "You'll get there." He slid two fingers into her.

Kandace busted through the door with the .9 in her right hand. She had a mug on her face. "How could you do this shit to me, Stevo?" She screamed.

Stevo hopped off of the bed. "Kandace, get yo monkey ass out of here. I'm handling my business."

"Fuck that. You choosing this ho to be yo bottom bitch over me. Really? After what we did to my sister!" She aimed the gun at Sasha.

Sasha tried to hide behind the pillow. She was too drunk off of Stevo's dick to understand that the bullets would go right through the pillow. "Please, Kandace. You can have him. I can't hang anyway. He's too much for me."

"Bitch, you should've thought about that before you fucked him." Kandace returned.

"Bitch, gimme the gun and get out of this room!" Stevo ordered.

"Fuck that!" Kandace rushed the bed, pulling the trigger of the gun. *Click! Click! Click! Click!* She stopped and looked at the barrel pulling the trigger again and again. "What the fuck?"

Sasha jumped from the bed and tackled her to the floor. They wrestled. Grunting loudly. They rolled around the carpet until Kandace wound up on top of Sasha. "Bitch, you wanna take my slot? You gotta kill me." She headbutt her as hard as she could.

Sasha felt the blow from her head and went dizzy. She released her grip on Kandace and tried to come from under her. "Get off of me, bitch."

Kandace was having none of it. She pressed the barrel of the gun to Sasha's head and pulled the trigger over and over again. The gun was empty. She smacked Sasha with it and threw it to the side. "Bitch, count yo blessings. Dis mafucka empty." She grabbed her by the throat. "You are under me. I'm the bottom bitch, and don't you ever forget it. If I even catch vying for my spot again, I'm smoking you. Do you hear me?" She screamed.

"Yes!" Sasha choked.

"Good!" She stood up and walked over to Stevo. "Nigga, I know you a killa. I know how you get down in these streets. But I don't give no fuck. You gon' respect me. I ain't Keaira, do you understand me?"

Stevo laughed. "Yeah, awright." He cocked back and knocked her clean out with one blow. She fell to the ground, snoring loudly. "Y'all come in here and clean up this mess." He ordered Carmen, and Sasha. Sasha had run into the hallway to get as far away from Kandace as she could.

Chapter 15

JaMichael stepped out of his black BMW into the night. He stuffed his black .40 Glock into his waistband and closed his suit jacket concealing his weapon. There was a light breeze that felt good to him coming from the east. He took a deep breath and blew it out. He felt the remnants of the Promethazine coursing through his system. His eye lids were heavy.

Makaroni came beside him double strapped. He had two twin .9 millimeters, and a chip on his shoulder. He looked across the street at the small barbecue shack. "Bruh, tell me why we finna sit down and holler at one of this nigga OGs instead of going directly at his head? I feel like we wasting time."

JaMichael shook his head. "This Memphis, bruh. Every nigga out here doing anythang got a mafuckin OG that they answer to. Phoenix ain't no different. Hopefully, this fool Bandos can talk some sense into his homeboy? My father brought the Rebirth to Memphis. His and his homie Tywain. By lineage, I'm supposed to be the one that this drug is passed down to. This nigga gotta honor my slot. He can either fall under me, or he can move around altogether, but he can't do both."

"So, what you think this old head finna do?" Makaroni asked as they walked across the street.

"Only thing I can hope for is that he can talk some sense into his lil' homie. If not, then we gon' have to buss his brain."

"Still seem like we wasting time. But aiight. This yo city. We gon' do shit yo way. I'ma follow you until I can't no more."

"That's all I ask." JaMichael opened the door to Mark's Barbecue Shack. Bells jingled to signify that new customers were arriving into the establishment. JaMichael walked right

up to the counter and smiled at the heavyset light skinned woman that stood behind it, ready to take his order. "How are you doing, sistah?"

"I'm fine, baby. And yo self?" She had a strong sexy southern drawl that Makaroni picked up on right away.

"I'm here to meet, Bandos. I suppose there is a room or somethin' in the back where we are supposed to be having dis meeting at?"

"Hold on, love. Let me go back hurr and see what he wanna do." She held up a finger and disappeared through the double doors that led to the kitchen.

Makaroni scanned the shop. The lights were dim. It looked to him as if the entire restaurant was made out of wood. The tables, the benches, the floors were all wood. There was strong stench of sweet barbecue coming from the back that smelled like paradise to him. His stomach growled. He did the best he could to ignore it. The restaurant was only lightly filled with patrons.

The yellow sistah came from the back with a broad smile on her face. "Baby, hurr he come right now. If thurr is any-thang dat I can personally do fo you fo you leave, make sho you let me know." She winked at JaMichael.

JaMichael laughed. "Will do, sistah."

Bandos came through the double doors. He was five feet ten inches tall. He was bald in the middle of his head. He had gray hair along the side of it. He waved to both JaMichael and Makaroni. "Y'all bring ya ass." He ordered.

JaMichael stepped behind the counters and followed the older man with Makaroni in tow. "What's good, old head?"

Bandos shook his head. "Same 'ol same 'ol shit. I'm trying to figure out when you young bucks gon' get it together?" He led them into the back office of the restaurant. It was small, and cramped. "Y'all sit right over there."

JaMichael took a seat inside of a hard-wooden chair that creaked as soon as he sat down. "Look, Bandos this shit is real simple. Dat nigga Phoenix gotta move around or else we finna have to go to war with some real devilish people. I ain't talking about no broke ass block boys either. I'm talking about some major muthafuckas. Now, he making this hustle shit hard for all of us."

Bandos listened with an attentive ear. He nodded over to Makaroni. "Who is dis?"

JaMichael looked at Makaroni. "Dis my lil' cousin. He from the north."

"North Memphis?" Bandos inquired.

"N'all, mane, up north by Illinois and where dem Green Bay Packers and shit play football. You know that team that Lil' Wayne like."

Bandos nodded. "Say, mane, what you doing all da way down chea?" His accent was just as southern as the yellow woman.

"Minding my business. I'm grown as a muthafucka, bruh." Makaroni hated nosey people. That included Bandos.

Bandos sucked his teeth. "Yeah, aiight potna. Anyway, dat same shit dat you just said to me JaMichael is damn near word for word what yo cousin said to me. Sounds like y'all are two different countries fighting over the same oil. You feel like you should have it because it was created by yo daddy. He feel like he should have it because he took over Memphis by use of that Rebirth product shortly after yo daddy got indicted. He don't feel like he should have to relinquish any ground just because you are Taurus's son."

"Yeah, well fuck that nigga, bruh. We can get this shit in blood den. What the fuck do you suggest?" JaMichael snapped.

Bandos scratched his bald spot. "This hurr restaurant is protected by the Duffel Bag Cartel. Anybody try to rob me, or my old lady up front durr, Phoenix and the Duffel Bag Cartel chop they ass up into little biddy pieces. What can you offer me?"

"What?" JaMichael was taken aback. "Fuck you mean, what can I offer you?"

"You want me to speak to Phoenix on your behalf. You want me to help squash y'all beef. Well, what's in it for me?" He took a pack of Kool cigarettes, and lit one.

The smoke gave Makaroni a migraine almost immediately. He hated the smell of nicotine or tobacco. When Bandos blew smoke in his direction, he felt like losing his cool. "Say bruh, blow that punk ass smoke somewhere else."

JaMichael fanned it easy. "What you want, old man?"

"In on the Rebirth. I got a few potnas back in Houston that's trying to do they lil' thang. They looking to set some shit up, but ain't got a consistent plug. I wanna be that plug if you take over Taurus's Rebirth."

"So you supposed to be Phoenix's OG, but you in here trying to make a back deal with us. Yet, we supposed to trust you to not stab us in the back when it becomes convenient for you? You got me fucked up." Makaroni snapped, unable to keep his cool.

"Yeah, Bandos. What type of shit is that?" JaMichael wanted to know.

"It's called business. Phoenix is my lil' homie but he still got a bunch of heat on him because of what he did to Mikey. It's a lot of people still plotting their revenge for that shiesty ass move. Mikey, in my opinion, was the original leader of the Duffel Bag Cartel. He had Memphis in order. Even with Dragon doing all of the shit he did in Black Haven."

"I don't give a fuck about none of that. Fuck Mikey. Fuck Phoenix. Fuck the Duffel Bag Cartel. Them niggas would've never been able to do none of the shit they did if it wasn't for my Pops. Memphis wouldn't be shit either. Them fuck niggas riding foreign whips and producing platinum rappers off of my Pop's creation. Mafuckas wouldn't even know what Memphis was if it wasn't for him."

Bandos laughed. "Boy, you got your facts all wrong. Your father didn't create the Rebirth. Hood Rich, and Meech did. Them boys are from Chicago. Your father linked up with them by way of some blond Russian named Nastia after your uncle Juice raped and kidnapped her. Taurus fell into good graces with her after he returned her safe and sound to her racist ass daddy. Because he did, she put him in with Hood Rich and Meech. They were the creators of the Rebirth. They flooded him with kilos, and that's how your daddy took over Memphis and a few surrounding states alike. The whole time he was doing his thang, Juice was trying to blow him off the face of the earth because he wanted to be the man. You see you Stevens have always tried to kill each other off for supremacy. Y'all done fucked up Memphis ever since you got hurr."

JaMichael got angry. He felt like he was being schooled. "Man, fuck yo history lesson. How you gon' get Phoenix to back down?"

"What's in it for me?" Bandos asked slyly.

"What?" JaMichael was getting irritated.

"You heard me. You thank I don't know that you warring with your cousin is a death sentence to the both of you right now? Boy, you better let me squash this shit." Bandos laughed. He took another toke from his cigarette.

"Awright, if you can squash shit, then I'll plug you into the Rebirth. You got my word on that." JaMichael agreed.

"Good. That sound like a plan. "Awright, give me a few weeks and I'll make it happen.

"A few weeks? We ain't got no few weeks. That shit gotta be done today or shit about to go down." Makaroni interrupted.

"Well, I don't know what to tell you other than you muthafuckas are screwed." He shrugged and sat back in his chair.

"A waste of muthafuckin time." Makaroni stood up, mugging the old man. "Yousa piece of shit, homie.

"Yeah, well in a few weeks you'll be fly food too. It is what it is. Y'all get the fuck out of my store." He waved them off.

"I told you, JaMichael. I told you dude bitch ass was a joke. We done spent all of that time talking to his sucka ass and we ain't got shit to show for it." Man, that was some bullshit." Makaroni wanted to say fuck JaMichael and head back to Milwaukee.

JaMichael walked across the parking lot in anger. First, Phoenix had set him up to be gunned down, and now he'd tried to have a peace talk with his OG and it had fallen through. He was irate. He was about to step across the street to get to his BMW when three black trucks came speeding down the street. Their headlights were off. He found that odd.

Makaroni's heart skipped a beat. He felt something bad was about to go down before it happened. He pulled both guns from his waistband and ran backward. "It's a hit, JaMichael."

The trucks were traveling with masked shooters sitting on the window of each one. They had fully automatics in their hands. Before the trucks came to a halt, they were firing at both Makaroni and JaMichael.

Boom. Boom. Boom. Boom.

Makaroni ran full speed to get behind a small red Buick. He ducked behind it as the enemy's bullets rocked the car

rapidly. He could smell the fire and gunpowder. He bussed his guns from the side of it.

Blocka! Blocka! Blocka! Blocka!

JaMichael found a minivan to get behind. He started shooting and counting as he bussed each shot. He wanted to make sure that he didn't run out of bullets. He didn't know who his attackers were, but he had a clue. This had the Duffel Bag Cartel and Phoenix written all over it. He felt like Bandos had set him up.

The trucks pulled into the parking lot shooting. Certain shooters aimed at JaMichael, while others looked to annihilate Makaroni. Bullet casings dropped to the pavement loudly. Gun smoke drifted to the sky. More and more shots were fired. Both JaMichael, and Makaroni appeared boxed in.

Bandos grabbed his old lady and fell to the floor with her as bullets ripped through the windows and shattered the store's front glass. His old lady had pressed the silent alarm to alert Phoenix and his Duffel Bag Cartel crew unbeknownst to Bandos. He held her tightly. "It's gone be okay, baby. All this shit will be over soon."

DaBaby jumped out of his rented Lincoln Town car with a hundred round Mach .90 that Jahliya had given him to roll around Memphis on security with. He rushed into the parking lot with Roscoe beside him. He peered through the scope and zoomed in the HD graphics to the driver of the first truck. He placed the aimer right on the side of his face and pulled the trigger.

Three bullets spit rapid from his machine gun. They tore into the driver's face and knocked muscles and tissues from him. His windshield filled with brain and blood. His truck crashed into the front of the restaurant creating a loud bang. DaBaby rushed the truck, still bucking.

Roscoe zoomed his scope into the driver of the second vehicle. He aimed for his neck. As soon as the scope lined up, he squeezed the trigger sending six shots his way. The bullets zipped across the parking lot and hit its mark. The driver's Adam's Apple was blown out of his throat along with his vocal chords. His foot slammed down on the gas of his truck. The truck hopped the curb and crashed into another car, exploding.

Makaroni took off running toward Roscoe. He bussed his guns at the enemies who were jumping out of the trucks and running in the other direction. When he got to Roscoe he slapped him on the shoulder. "Good shit, kinfolk. I owe you, nigga."

Roscoe nodded. "Get in the car." He ran toward the Duffel Bag Cartel shooting, planting big holes into their trucks.

JaMichael ran and jumped in the car seconds later. "Where the fuck you find these niggas?" He shouted.

"I didn't. Stevo did."

"That's what's up. I'll meet y'all back at the mansion." He jumped out of the car, and into his BMW. He stepped on the gas and pulled away, sending smoke into the air.

Makaroni watched DaBaby, and Roscoe go to work blowing the trucks up. They fell to the ground bussing their guns until the Duffel Bag Cartel fled in different directions. Phoenix watched the scenes unfold by use of security cameras that were attached to the barbecue joint. He nodded in excitement. "Oh yeah. Well, let's get it then." He quipped. He knew that there was going to be a deadly war looming up ahead. He was ready for it. He didn't believe that JaMichael could out smart him. He felt that he should've been the sole leader of the distribution of the Rebirth. He didn't care if JaMichael was Taurus's son or not.

Chapter 16

JaMichael put his arm around Makaroni's shoulder as they walked up and down the Bentley lot. "Look my nigga, I already know that we got a hell of a mission ahead of us. That don't mean that I can't look out for you, and your lil' homeboys for what they did a couple days ago. Them mafuckas saved our lives. The reason I'm hitting you the hardest is because you are their boss. You made the call for them to follow you down here to Memphis, and because you did, they yanked their business, and we are still alive." He waved his hand over the lot. "As a token of my appreciation, I want you to pick anythang off dis here lot, and it's yours. I mean any thang, too. The owner owes me more than a few favors." JaMichael smiled. The sunlight reflected off of his pearly white teeth. There was a small gap in the upper row.

"Cuz, you ain't gotta get me no Bentley for my boys handling their business. That's what we came down here for. Besides, all this time that we spending here we could be out looking for Phoenix and his crew."

"N'all, nigga. Fuck that. Dis is Memphis, homeboy. Down here, we show our appreciation by blowing that bag. Running up a check. Now, we ain't leaving this here lot until you snatch up something exclusive. If I was you, I'd roll back to the Mill in one of these newly released Bentley trucks. Check this black on black one out right here." They walked over to a red newly released 2020 Bentley Bentayga. "Now this mafucka right here will have you killing shit. Its turbo charged. Three liters with a V6 engine, and it's a hybrid. You can't ask for a better foreign whip than this one. It cost a pretty penny, but it ain't nothing to a boss. That's exactly what you are, a boss. Especially, when we knock this nigga Phoenix out of the equation."

Makaroni shook his head. He didn't care about what truck he was driving, especially since it seemed as if he wouldn't be driving it for long if they didn't crush Phoenix soon. He simply wanted to get off of the lot, and back to the mansion where they could plan Phoenix's hit. "Fuck it cuz, wrap this bitch up in black on black. Make sure I got that red leather interior, and we good to go."

JaMichael threw his arm around his shoulder. "Now, that's what I'm talking about. And don't worry about yo homeboys. They riding back to Milwaukee in Benzs. I owe them lil' niggas."

"Yeah, and I'm pretty sure that before it's all said and done we gone owe them some more. Let's get this whip and get up out of here."

***

Stevo leaned his head down to the mirror and tooted a line of the Rebirth into his right nostril hard. Then, he did the left one. He pinched his nose and leaned his head back against the cushions of the couch. The drug took over his senses, and gave him a body high almost immediately. He closed his eyes with a smile spread across his face. In front of him was five hundred thousand dollars in cash that needed to be counted. Stevo didn't use money machines until he had the girls count his cash by hand. After they finished, he ran each bill through a money counter to confirm their totals. If ever one was off by so much as a hundred dollars, he would whoop their asses with no mercy. He would be stressing the importance of getting his totals right. He ran his tongue over his teeth and smacked his lips.

Kandace stepped from the kitchen with a big butcher's knife in her hand. She gripped the handle of the knife tight. She stepped into the living room with her heart beating fast. As the days went on, she began to hate Stevo. He showed her

less and less attention. He seemed more consumed with Sasha, and Carmen than he did her. She didn't understand why he treated her the way that he did. She couldn't fathom why he preferred the other girls more than he did her. She had given him her virginity. She had been loyal to him to a fault. She had even betrayed her own sister, and because of her betrayal, her sister was now deceased. She would think that a sacrifice like that would have made Stevo love her with a boundless set of unconditional love, but it had been quite the opposite. Because of her treatment, she resented him, and she hated herself. She hated herself for being so weak. She disliked the reflection of her face in the mirror. Whenever she closed her eyes, she saw Keaira crying out to her. Keaira cried and asked her what would make her do what she'd done. Kandace woke up in cold sweats only to see that the bedroom was empty of her friends. She would be awakened to the sounds of their passionate moans or their laughter that they shared with Stevo. She felt so alone and connecting with her mother was an impossible task as well. Stevo had gotten her hooked on the Rebirth. Now, she didn't care what Kandace did or about the fact that Stevo was screwing her teen daughter. She had yet to ask Kandace where Keaira and Steven were. Kandace was oblivious to the fact that Stevo had killed her nephew. She just never thought to inquire about him. She stayed away from home as much as she could now. The sight of the house, or even being on the same block as the house made her feel sick.

She clutched the handle tighter. Her heart pounded in her chest. I'm finna just do it. She thought. I'm finna kill his selfish ass and get it over with. It's his fault that Keaira dead. He got me hooked on these drugs. If he would've never came into my room that day, kissing all on me, this would've never happened. I hate him so much. She crept closer to the couch. The courage within her, was building with each step that she took.

She had to do it. She needed to. She had to enact revenge for Keaira. She had to make things right with the universe. She got as close to Stevo as she could. She took a deep breath and raised the knife over her head. She got ready to bring it down to end his life, and the pain that he had created deep within her soul. There was no turning back. She frowned her face and prepared for the impact. The ripping of his skin from the puncturing of the blade.

Carmen was on her way to the bathroom when she looked down the hallway and saw Kandace with the knife raised over her head. "Kandace!" Carmen yelled.

Kandace jumped back and lowered the knife. She tucked it in front of her as to shield it from the sights of Carmen. She slowly backed away from Stevo. He nodded on the couch, scratching himself. He mumbled under his breath. His words were incoherent.

Carmen met her halfway. "Girl, what are you doing?" She whispered.

Kandace looked back over her shoulder at Stevo. Her heart was still racing. She grabbed a hold of Carmen's wrist and pulled her into the back bedroom. She glanced down the hallway toward Stevo one final time before she closed the door.

"Girl, what the hell is going on? Were you about to kill him?" Carmen asked fearful. She had heard whispers about Kandace supposing to have had something to do with Keaira's disappearance. She didn't really believe the rumors, but now that she'd saw Kandace with a knife raised over her head seeming as if she was getting ready to kill Stevo, she wasn't so sure.

"Carmen, you don't understand what his punk ass done put me through."

"So, you was finna kill him? Holy shit. Did you really have somethin' to do with Keaira's disappearance?" Carmen

blurted. She needed to know what kind of monster she was dealing with.

"What? No. Of course not." Kandace lied. "That is my sister. I love her. What would make you ask me something like that?"

"Bitch, because you were holding a knife over our Daddy's head like you were getting ready to take his life. If you kill him, then how are we going to survive?" She sniffed and pulled her nose. She felt her sickness coming on. She was feening for the Rebirth.

"Shush, girl. Wasn't nobody finna kill his ass. Stop saying that shit before you get me in trouble." She tiptoed back to the door, peeking out of it. Sasha was easing to the floor. She pulled out Stevo's dick and started to give him some well-trained head. Kandace closed the door back. "Girl, we need to get out of here."

"What? Where the fuck are we going to go? We ain't got no money. Stevo pays for everything. He supplies all of our needs, and all of us are hooked on his dope. We need him." She felt her stomach turn upside down. She felt sick. The Rebirth was calling for her in the worst way.

"Carmen, you are only sixteen. You can't be throwing your life away for a man. We can still be something great. We need to get away from him while we still got a chance."

"Bitch, you tripping. I got it made here. I don't pay no rent. I don't pay no bills period. My daddy ain't all in my face every time he get drunk. My mama ain't smoking dope in front of me. My clothes are clean. I stay high all day, and that grown meat that he handing down ain't too shabby neither. What's the matter with you today? You on yo period or somethin'?" Carmen turned her head sideways questioning.

"N'all. Look, he don't care about us. You might think you ain't paying no bills but every time you lay on yo back, where does the money go?"

"To my Daddy."

"Bitch, he ain't yo daddy. He yo pimp. Daddy's don't treat their little girls like he do." Kandace was getting frustrated.

"Mine sure as hell didn't. He treated me worse than Stevo do. Hell, he treated me worse than any one of those men that I sleep with for money treat me. At least, they don't beat my ass. So, if you think I'm finna go back to that hellhole then you got another thing coming. Get out of my way. I'm finna tell him what yo crazy ass was finna do." She went to grab the knob of the door.

Kandace smacked her hand away. "Wait a minute, Carmen. What if I could offer you a better life then he can?"

"Girl, if you don't get yo simple ass out my way, I'm finna scream. Now move."

Kandace blocked her path. "Wait a minute, Carmen. Now I'm the one that brought you into this mess. I wanna be the one to pull you out. Please hear me out."

Carmen's head was pounding. She wanted the Rebirth. She was sick for it. Her vision was slowly starting to go blurry. "Kandace, I'm getting really sick right now. I can barely see. If you don't get out of my way, I am going to scream. Now move. I'm finna tell Stevo everything you just said to me with yo jealous ass. You just mad cause he don't want you no more. He get tired of the bitches in your family real quick. Even yo hype ass mama."

Kandace was stunned by her disrespect. "Excuse me?"

Carmen, irritated by her need for the Rebirth, and Kandace blocking her path wanted to hurt Kandace as much as she could so she could get the hint to leave her alone.

"Yeah, bitch that's right. Sasha told me everything. Stevo fucked you, Keaira, and y'all mama. He say the pussy ain't so good in y'all family. That's why he been kicking yo ass to the curb. Now get the fuck out of my way. You has been."

Kandace felt her temper boiling. "Say dat shit again."

Carmen frowned. "Bitch, yousa has been, now move." She grabbed a handful of Kandace's hair, and yanked her head so hard that she made her neck pop.

"Let me go." Kandace swung the knife and implanted it into Carmen's stomach. She forced it upward, and pulled it back out.

Carmen felt the blade puncture her stomach. Then, it traveled upwards so far until it came to a forcible stop. The blade came out with her blood attached to it. She held her stomach and pushed Kandace away from her. She reached for the doorknob.

Kandace snapped. "Aw, no you don't." She stabbed her in the back as hard as she could three times. "I. Tried. To. Save yo ass, bitch. Then, you say some shit like that?"

Carmen fell to her knees and crawled across the floor. She plopped to her bleeding stomach. "Why, Kandace?" She croaked. "Why did you do this?"

Kandace was in another killer mind state. She felt nothing for Carmen. When she looked at her, she saw Stevo. She hated them both. She knelt down and stabbed her repeatedly until her arm went weak. Then, she switched hands and stabbed her some more. When she finished, she stood up and looked down on her. There was blood everywhere. She could hear Sasha moaning and screaming in the living room. She knew that they would be in there for a minute. She grabbed the blankets off of the bed, and wrapped Carmen in them. She rolled her up, and into the closet. Then, she got dressed. She snuck into Stevo's room and grabbed five thousand dollars in cash, and

an ounce of the Rebirth. She climbed out of the back window and ran as fast as she could down the alley.

Chapter 17

Bandos twirled Kathy around in a circle and dipped her as the Isley Brothers played through the speakers in the Marcy Lounge. He was tipsy off of a half of bottle of Crown Royal, and two lines of the Rebirth. He pulled Kathy to him and kissed her neck. "Tonight is going to be amazing, baby. You know that, don't you?"

"Long as you continue to make it all about me, it sho is." She laughed and turned her back to him. She grooved in his lap. "Hold me tight now, lil' daddy." She wiggled her hips from side to side.

Bandos held her tighter and licked her neck. "Yeah, it's gon' be mighty fine tonight. I'm looking forward to it." He swung her back around until her arms were around his neck.

DaBaby pulled his black hood over his head and crept into the backdoor of the Lounge. He took a second before he allowed for the door to close, to peek into the night to make sure that he wasn't being followed. After confirming that he wasn't, he stepped into the back door. He was met with the stench of tobacco, and alcohol. He could feel the Codeine coursing through his system, along with the three Percocet Sixties that he'd popped before he left the mansion. He balled his hands into fists, to flex his fingers. They were feeling numb. When the feeling came back, he tucked them into his black Marc Jacobs.

The Lounge had only a few customers that were dancing in pairs. The owner had moonlighting on. The Isley Brothers crooned through the speakers.

"Groove with you." They sang while the patrons swayed their hips to the melody. DaBaby eyed the dance floor like a lethal hunter. In seconds, he found both Bandos and Kathy dancing closer to the juke box. Bandos had his hands all over

the heavyset light skinned woman's backside while he sucked on her neck. DaBaby took out his phone to compare the frozen pictures of each target. Once confirmed, he replaced the phone. He pulled his hoody tighter and slid on a bar stool.

A dark skinned, pretty faced, bartender stepped up to serve him. "What will you be dranking tonight, baby?" She asked with her most winning smile.

"Let me get a shot of Grey Goose. Matter of fact make that two shots. How long y'all stay open?" He asked eyeing Bandos and Kathy.

"Oh, we close at three in the morning. That's about forty-five minutes from now. Why you ask that?" She poured the drink that he asked for.

DaBaby slapped a twenty on the bar. "No reason. I'm just going through some thangs. I wanted to know how long I had to drink my sorrows away. That's all."

She smiled. "Well baby, you got forty-one minutes now. I'll keep em' coming."

***

"You gon' sit in here all day? Or are you gon' come downstairs and kick it with everybody else?" Jahliya asked Makaroni after sticking her head into the door of the guestroom she was allowing him to use. She stepped all the way inside of the room, and softly closed the door behind her.

Makaroni was laid on his back looking at the ceiling. "Man, I just been lost in my thoughts."

Jahliya came and laid on the bed next to him. She looked over at his handsome face. "Care to share?"

"Cuz, I don't know if I want this life." He kept his eyes pinned on a spot that was stuck in the ceiling.

"What do you mean?"

148

"Well, the way I see it, is the only way we'll ever be able to live like bosses, or keep plenty gwap is if we destroy each other, or our community. I was just laying here thinking like that shit ain't cool. The way that Rebirth is fuckin' up Milwaukee is wild. More kids are losing their parents, and at the same time, we are hooking the shorties, too. I got so many bodies under my belt now that I can't sleep at night. Every time I go to cop something fresh, whether it be a fit, a piece a jewelry, or a whip, I think about how many mafuckas I had to put down to get to where I am. Now shit so bad that we gotta kill somebody from our own bloodline in order to flourish. I don't know how yo pops really was, but I know this ain't the vision he had for the Rebirth."

Jahliya sighed. "This is the Game you signed up for though, Makaroni. Dis shit ain't all peaches and cream. It's a lot of good that comes along with it, but there is also a lot of bad. There will be bloodshed, and a bunch of lives will be lost. That's the cost you gotta pay in order to stand on top of everybody else. I made my peace with that a long time ago."

"But how do you do it, though? How do you sleep at night knowing that you got this mansion off of bloodshed?"

"Like a baby, to be honest with you. This ain't the life I chose for myself. I was born into this. My mother conceived me in this dope game. She conceived me in blood. I can't see myself living like a bum. I can't do the broke shit. I gotta drive the latest. I gotta have my hair, my nails, my toes, and everything with me, top notch. I'm a boss bitch. I can't help that. My parents put this DNA in me." She sat up. "Nigga, it's too late to be in here sulking like a bitch. Fuck those soft feelings that you are feeling right now because they don't matter. The only thing that does matter is us finding Phoenix and annihilating his ass. Once he took out of the game, then we can all go on with our lives."

Makaroni nodded. "You can watch yo mafuckin' mouth, too. Ain't shit soft about me. I'm just thinking over some things. That's all."

"Yeah, well think that shit over once you master your mission. Killas think while they are performing their tasks of attack. You laying here convincing yourself that you are doing something wrong. You weren't sent here to save humanity. You can only get yo slice of the pie while you're down here. When you get to hell, you gon' have to find a way to come up out of that mafucka, too. Everything is about levels. It's either you gon' be a man, or a bitch. With all this meat, I pray that you choose man." She gripped his dick and squeezed it.

Makaroni knocked her hand away. Montana crossed his mind. "Like I said before, I'm choosing you and JaMichael. You ain't gotta worry about that. But once this shit is all said and done, I'ma take a different route with the Rebirth. I can't keep hurting so many mafuckas for my own selfish gains. That part of our bloodline ain't in me."

Jahliya stood up and pulled her skirt up. She straddled his lap. She had a thick thigh on either side of him. "Aw, you got that humanitarian shit in you?" She leaned down, and sucked his neck.

"I guess I do. I mean I don't know what I'ma do yet. But it's gone be more than just being a dope boy."

Jahliya slid her hand into his boxers. "Cuz, once we kill Phoenix you gone be much more than a dope boy. You gon' be a Drug Lord. We already agreed that we giving you a few cities. You finna be making more money than you will know what to do with. You can do whatever you want with it. It's yours." She kissed down his neck and pulled his dick out of his pants. She pumped it. "Damn, cuz you got a big dick. I see these definitely run in the family." She pumped it for a minute. Then, she sucked it into her mouth.

150

Makaroni guided her head. Her mouth was hot and wet. Her tongue swirled around the head. She sucked hard until he was moaning. "Damn, cuz. Slow down."

She popped him out of her mouth. "Why baby. What, you can't handle this shit?" She rested her hands on his stomach and sucked him at full speed, making smacking noises. Her mouth came off of him. She licked up and down his length. "I love our family. Fuck, I do."

Makaroni pushed her off of him. He stood up and got behind her. He yanked her skirt up to her lower back and pulled her boy shorts to the middle of her knees. He slid into her pussy with one stroke, fucking her as hard as he could. Her ass jiggled while he pounded her out. "I missed this pussy. Fuck, I did."

Jahliya frowned and humped back into him. "I know cuz. I know." She closed her eyes and balled the blanket into her right fist while she beat on the bed with her left. Her mouth was wide open. She moaned loudly and relished in his thick dick going in and out of her.

JaMichael was walking down the hallway when he heard Jahliya emit a moan that sounded like she was in pain. He stopped in his tracks and jogged toward the noise. He stopped outside of the guestroom and twisted the knob. He pushed in the door. It took a second for his eyes to adjust to what he was seeing. Makaroni held Jahliya by the hips, long stroking her. He actually saw his cousin's dick coming nearly all of the way out before it slammed back into her over and over. Jahliya groaned and threw her ass back into him hungry for the dicking. JaMichael was in disbelief. He didn't know what to do.

**

Bandos slipped his button up off of his arms and allowed for it to drop to the floor. He unbuckled his white leather belt.

His pants fell to his ankles. He kicked them away. "Mama, I'm finna wear that big ass out. You finna get all of this cat daddy tonight."

Kathy opened her red robe and exposed her black negligee underneath. She tossed the robe on to the floor. "I guess you thank since you wined and dined me, you get to lay me down, huh?"

Bandos hooked his thumbs into his boxers and pulled them down and off. His piece hung low. "Dat sound like what I had in mind. You got other plans or somethin?"

Kathy snickered. "N'all, Daddy'o, you want it you gotta come and get it." She bent over the bed and slapped her ass cheeks. The smack resonated through the room.

Bandos was hard as a block of wood. He loved big girls, and he loved Kathy even more than that. He hurried to the bed and stuck his face right into her middle. He sniffed hard. He could smell her sweat, and the scent of her pussy. They had been dancing all night so her parts smelling a bit was to be expected. It drove him crazy. Bandos sucked her sweat through the panties. Then, he pulled the crotch away so he could see her meaty lips. "Hell yeah." He went to work eating away as if he were starving.

Kathy moaned and held herself open for him. "Get it Daddy'o. All of it. Unn-shit yeah."

DaBaby slipped from the closet, and tiptoed over to Bandos. He turned the gun around so that he was holding the barrel. He raised it over his head and brought it down as hard and as fast as he could. Clunk! The handle took a chunk out of Bandos' forehead. He fell on the floor with blood gushing out of the hole.

Kathy jumped up with her drawers around her ankles. She tried to pull them up. "Please. I don't know what he did. But please don't take it out on me."

152

Boom. Boom. Boom.

Kathy felt the bullets rip into her skull, before her brains flew out the back of her head. She started to stutter as she fell to the carpet shaking. Her eyes crossed. Her legs continued to kick like crazy.

DaBaby stood over her. He aimed for her forehead again. *Boom. Boom.*

Bandos stood up with blood running down his face. "What do you want, man? What do you want?"

"Where is Phoenix?" DaBaby asked slamming another clip into his .45.

"Phoenix? I don't know, man. Did you check Orange Mound?"

Boom.

A bullet shattered his left knee cap. He knelt down like Colin Kapernick. Blood spilled out of the wound. He struggled to stand back up.

"Where is Phoenix?" DaBaby stood over him with murderous intent.

"Awright, man. He stay out in White Haven. He got a nice lil' place over on Sycamore Road. Third mini mansion from the right. Address 2317 Sycamore Plaza. He got two lil' girls, and a wife. That's everything man. Please, let me go." Bandos whimpered.

DaBaby stood over him in disgust. "Where is your loyalty nigga?" He aimed at his face and gave him ten shots. The bullets ate away his mug like hungry Lions in the wild. DaBaby wiped his face with the back of his hand. Bandos blood had popped up on him. "Snitch ass nigga." He pulled out his phone and snapped pictures of both bodies, before leaving them in a puddle of blood.

***

Jahliya damn near screamed as she looked into the face of JaMichael. She pushed away from Makaroni and jumped up with cum running down her inner thigh. "JaMichael, I can explain."

JaMichael stood there furious. He nodded. "So, how long y'all been fuckin'?"

Jahliya held up her hands. "Just a few times. It ain't nothing serious. We was just having a lil' fun."

Makaroni stood up and pulled his boxers in place. "Nigga, so what. We fuckin'. What's the big deal? I already know y'all get down with each other, too."

JaMichael looked at Jahliya shocked. "You been telling this nigga our business, too?"

"I ain't told him shit. But he ain't got no room to talk. He fuckin' Montana. Ain't nobody innocent in this room." Jahliya shot back.

"Man, fuck all that. I ain't came yet. That pussy was just getting good. We can do all that arguing and shit after I cum in her thick ass. You got a problem wit' that JaMichael, we can box later." Makaroni grabbed Jahliya to him. He gripped her juicy ass. His dick began to rise.

She tried to push away from his chest. "Stop, Makaroni. I ain't trying to have JaMichael mad at me."

Makaroni rubbed her pussy. "Shid, we both already fuckin. What's the big deal? As thick as she is, we can both fuck her. Keep this shit in the family fa real."

Jahliya felt her pussy get wetter from the thought of getting flipped by the two of them. "I ain't no ho. Y'all ain't finna treat me like one either." She fronted.

JaMichael watched how Makaroni rubbed all over Jahliya's box and became aroused. "Nigga, you know what? Montana gave me a hard time when she was down here. She

wasn't trying to let me fuck. If we buss down Jahliya, you owe me the same treatment with Montana. Deal."

"Montana grown as hell. That's on her." He slid two fingers into Jahliya. She was dripping wet, "but yo sis ready right now. What's good?"

JaMichael stood watching Jahliya for a minute. He turned on his toes and locked the door. "You can't fuck wit' my business when it comes to her and I'm finna show you why."

Ghost

Chapter 18

Jahliya scooted back on the bed until her back was resting against the headboard. "JaMichael, you sure we finna do this in front of him?"

JaMichael dropped his Polo boxers to the ground and climbed in the bed. "We family anyway. What's to hide?"

Makaroni laid on his side. He snuck his hand between Jahliya's thick thighs and rubbed her box. It was leaking worse than he had ever seen it leaking before. He could tell that she was turned on. She spaced her feet. He slipped two fingers deep into her box.

Jahliya felt the insertion and moaned. JaMichael kissed her lips, licking all over them. His tongue slipped past her lips to wrestle with that of his own. She moaned again. "What are y'all finna do to me?"

JaMichael kissed her sexy lips harder. "I'm finna show lil' cuz that he can't fuck wit' my business when it comes to this pussy. He think shit sweet." He unloosened her bra in the front. Her breasts came spilling out of the cups. He held them up. His thumbs went back and forth across her nipples. They were erect and ready to be sucked.

Makaroni began to finger her faster. Her sex lips were open like the petals of a rose. Her pink interior flashed over and over each time he pulled them out to far. Her juices dripped off of the side of his hand. "I'm finna kill this shit."

Jahliya whimpered. She shivered. Goosebumps came all over her skin. She couldn't believe that she was about to let them double team her. While there was a voice in her head that told her not to do it, her pussy screamed for her to go through with it.

JaMichael held her face while they made out. "I love you beautiful. But you belong to me. Cuz might be playing wit' that pussy, but I own that pussy down there. You hear me?"

She nodded, and yelped. "Fuck."

Makaroni pulled her away from JaMichael and laid her on her side. "I told you I ain't came yet." He ran his piece head up and down her slit until he sunk in. As soon as his piece dove into her wetness, he proceeded to fuck her. He grabbed her hips and pounded away.

Jahliya closed her eyes. "Mmm. Mmm. Fuck cuz. Its. Its. Shit!" She had to hold on to the side of the bed because Makaroni was fucking her so hard. "Awww, you killing me."

Makaroni wasn't trying to hear none of that. He watched his dick going in and out of Jahliya. Her small hole could barely suck in the width of him. Her lips puckered out only to suck back inward. She was drooling her secretions.

JaMichael stroked his piece. He guided her face into his lap. "Get me ready so I can show dis nigga what it is."

Jahliya moaned. "Shit! Cuz!" She squeezed her eyelids together and came hard pushing back into Makaroni. She trembled. She grabbed JaMichael's dick and sucked him into her mouth. Now that she had came, she was hungry for more. She deep throated him like a pro.

JaMichael played with her hard nipples. He pulled them and cuffed her entire right breast. He did the same with the left. "You so fine, Jahliya. I swear to God you so perfect, sis." He ran his fingers through her curls while she sucked him loudly.

Makaroni stroked her harder. He pulled all the way back and slammed forward. Then, he was fuckin her as fast as he could. He felt the pressure mounting in his balls. Her inner walls sucked at him. He jerked. She bounced back into his lap.

158

He saw the way her ass jiggled and couldn't hold back. "I'm cuming! Fuck! I'm cuming." He squirted off in her.

Jahliya released JaMichael from her mouth and screamed. She ran her tongue all over her lips. "Fuck, it feel so good. He cuming a lot." She bounced back into him over and over until he pulled out.

JaMichael flipped her on her back and got between her thighs. He laid on top of her, and sucked her nipples, one at a time. He knew that one of Jahliya's weak spots were her nipples. They were ultra-sensitive. The blowing of the wind, or the way her shirts brushed against her nipples could easily cause for her to have an orgasm.

"Unn. Unn. JaMichael. Baby."

JaMichael pulled on her big nipples with his lips. He sucked just right. His teeth lightly scraped them, then he was sucking again. He opened her pussy lips, took his thumb and rotated it around her clitoris.

Jahliya humped into his hand. It felt so good. She felt like she was exploding through her nipples. Her cream ran down and into her ass crack. "I'm finna cum, JaMichael. I'm finna cum. You know how my nipples are!" She screamed and came with a double earth shattering orgasm. Her thighs locked up. She dug her nails into his shoulder blades and hugged him to her.

JaMichael looked over at Makaroni with a smile on his face. He knew how to make Jahliya come in more ways than any man could ever understand. He didn't care about their relation. In his mind, Jahliya belonged to him first, then came everybody else. He pushed her titties together, and made love to her nipples for another few minutes. He only focused on them. By the time he sat back up, Jahliya had cum three times and she was out of breath. Her clit was super sensitive.

Makaroni watched the lips of her pussy puff up even more. He wanted to fuck her again. Her scent was driving him out of his mind. She was so thick. Her thighs jiggled every time she moved them. That enticed him.

JaMichael pushed her knees to her chest. He slipped into her. "This how you fuck Jahliya." He cocked back and began pumping with all of his might. His long piece stroked her G spot at every stab. He could feel her juices leaking all over him. He started to grunting.

"Uh. Uh. JaMichael. Wait. Shit. Bruh. Wait. My pussy. Uhhhh!" She closed her eyes while he dug her out in brute fashion. It felt so good to Jahliya that she bit into his shoulder and screamed. She knew who it was on top of her and it drove her crazy. He was fucking her. She was giving him the pussy. It was so wrong, and broke so many rules, but she craved the taboo in it all. Every time she felt him touch her stomach, she screamed.

JaMichael didn't know how much longer he could hold back. Jahliya's pussy was always so good to him. Her scent. Her tightness. Their relation. It was all too much. He dropped her knees from her chests and leaned down so he could kiss all over her lips. He humped forward and came over and over. "Shit. Shit. Jahliya! Baby!"

Jahliya opened her thighs wide. She felt him stroking her and loved every second of the pounding. She wrapped her ankles around his lower back and came licking his chest.

JaMichael pulled out, and drug her to the edge of the bed. He stood up and put her on all fours. Once there, he fingered her rosebud slowly at first. He gradually picked up speed. She was tight. He used her kitty juices to lube her.

Jahliya opened her thighs wide and slid down to her elbows. Her fat ass was spread open for JaMichael to do with of

160

what he pleased. She knew what came next, and she was yearning for it.

JaMichael slipped into her box for five strokes. He pulled out with his piece covered in her fluids. He pressed his head on her rose bud, and pushed in. The tightness made him want to cum.

Jahliya ran her tongue all over her juicy lips. She had a habit of doing this whenever she was at her horniest point. "Fuck me, JaMichael. Tear that ass up back there."

JaMichael slammed forward implanting himself deep within her bowels. He took a hold of her cheeks and rocked back and forth inside of her. "Gimme. Dis. Sis. Dis. My body. Mine. Mine. Mine. Fuck. Mine!" He growled through clenched teeth.

Jahliya beat on the bed with her fist. Whenever she let Ja-Michael tap her ass, she couldn't control herself from coming prematurely back to back. She loved when he staked his claim over her. It did something to her that she couldn't understand. She slammed back on him thirty hard times while she fondled her clit and came screaming how much she loved him.

JaMichael flipped her over and fell between her thighs again. He slid back into her ass fucking her with moderate deep strokes. "You. Belong. To. Me." He reiterated.

Makaroni slowly eased out of the room. JaMichael had made his point. He saw that he didn't have any win with Jahliya. She belonged to JaMichael and that's just what it was. Their bond was too strong. Besides, Makaroni didn't care about penetrating their bond as long as he could continue to fuck Jahliya whenever he wanted to; that was all that mattered to him. She was too fine for him to give up that fight. He didn't care how JaMichael felt about it. He jumped into the shower with Montana on his brain.

Ghost

***

Montana was on her way to Stevo's trap when she saw Kandace running down busy 27th Street. Kandace was out of breath. She kept looking over her shoulder, running as fast as she could. Montana blew the Lexus horn twice to get her attention. Kandace looked out and see Montana's Lexus and tried to run faster. She didn't know if Stevo had already found Carmen and he was looking for her. She wanted to get as far away from him and anybody that knew him as she could.

Montana switched lanes and pulled closer to the curb. "Kandace! Kandace! Girl, you hear me calling you!" She shouted.

Kandace's heart was pounding. She couldn't breathe. She rested up against the side of a corner store located on 27th and Brown. "I ain't going back. I can't. I swear to God I will kill you if you try and make me." She hollered. She ran toward 26th.

Montana was dismayed. She stepped on the gas and sped up. When she got a few paces in front of Kandace, she threw her truck in park and jumped out. She caught up to a jogging Kandace quick. "Lil' sister. What's the matter? Where aren't you going back to?" Montana asked as the sun began to set bringing upon a breezy night chill.

Kandace knelt to one knee. "Stevo trying to kill me. He already killed my sister, and my friend Carmen cause she ain't wanna sell pussy for him no more." She lied. "Now he wanna kill me, too. I ain't selling myself. I refuse. I'm just a kid." She cried. She knew that her tears would help her to convince Montana. She saw that she was rolling a Lexus truck. She knew that she had to have some sort of money. Keaira had always told her that Montana and Stevo never got along. She wanted to use that to her advantage.

162

Montana knelt beside her. She was furious. "How do you know that Stevo killed your sister?" She asked in a soothing tone.

"Because he told me he did." She lied all the more. "He told me that every time he fucked me to scare me. I don't wanna die like her. I don't want him to stab me up like he did Carmen in front of me." She broke into a fit of fake tears.

Montana held her close. "Its okay baby. I promise you ain't never gotta worry about Stevo ever again. I got you."

***

Stevo stepped out of the shower and stretched his arms over his head. "Man, ain't nothin like some fresh ass pussy to get a muthafuckas night started. Now, it's time to get this money." He dried off and slipped on his boxers when Sasha screamed at the top of her lungs.

"Oh my God! Oh my God! Daddeee!" She screamed running down the hallway and to the bathroom.

Stevo grabbed her and shook her. "Bitch, why are you doing all of that mafuckin' screaming? Huh?"

Sasha burst into tears. "Somebody dead in the closet." She began to shake.

Stevo shook her again. "What the fuck you say?"

"Somebody wrapped up in the closet dead. Its blood everywhere."

He tossed her to the side. He took off running into the back room. He looked around. He saw the blood stains on the carpet right away. "Kandace! Bitch, where you at? Carmen? You hoes bet not be playin wit' me." He warned. He saw a puddle of blood coming from the closet. He opened the door and Carmen's body came rolling out of it. He jumped back and looked down. "What the fuck?" He knelt down and uncovered the body good enough so he could see the face. "Carmen. Son of

a bitch. Where is Kandace?" He knew right away that it had to be her. He felt angry. "Where is Kandace?" He hollered.

Sasha ran into the room and saw Carmen's face. She dropped to her knees and threw up. "Oh my God! She's dead! Kandace killed her." She guessed. She knew Kandace was crazy. She knew it couldn't have been anybody else.

Stevo grabbed her by her hair. "She didn't say nothing to you about where she was going? Huh?" He pulled harder.

"No. I swear she didn't. We ain't spoke in days.

"Bitch, go in there and get them cleaning supplies and clean up this mess. I'll get rid of Carmen. Then, I'ma find this ungrateful bitch. Now, go get what I told you to!" He slung her toward the hallway. Sasha landed on her knees crying. "Get up and do like I told you to before I gotta bury yo ass next. Go!"

"Okay." Sasha took off to follow his commands.

Stevo looked down on Carmen. Her eyes were wide open as if she were still in shock. He peeled opened the blanket and lifted her shirt. He saw the multiple stab wounds. He covered her back up and shook his head in disbelief.

"Fuck, that lil' bitch just as crazy as me." He laughed. He didn't know what else to do about the situation. One thing was for sure. Kandace had to die. She had caused him too many problems. It was the only solution that made sense.

Chapter 19

It was a dark and rainy day. The wind whistled loudly and sent the heavy rain down violently. Lightning flashed across the sky, followed by a roaring thunder. Two days after Montana found Kandace walking down 27th street, she pulled her Lexus truck up to Stevo's Trap house located on 25th and Kilbourne. She grabbed her purple umbrella and opened it before she stepped out into the rain. Lightning flashed across the sky, illuminating it. She felt hysterical. She had always hated thunderstorms. She rushed up the steps and beat on Stevo's door. *Bomp. Bomp. Bomp. Bomp.*

Stevo slid back from the table and cocked his .40 Glock. He jumped up with a bulletproof vest across his chest. He bolted to the front door and pulled back the curtain. The only thing he could see was Montana's big umbrella. He ran to the back of the house, and out the backdoor. Once there, he opened it and hopped over the neighbors' fence. He ran down their gangway and came out of the front of their house. He aimed his gun at Montana while she continued to knock at his Trap house door. His black beater was drenched in rain along with his dreadlocks. "Man, who the fuck is you standing on my porch?" He hollered.

Montana jumped back. She searched for the voice until she found Stevo with his gun pointed at her. "Boy. You scared the shit out of me." She placed her hand over her chest to emphasize her point. Her heart was beating fast.

Stevo lowered his gun. "Montana? Girl, what the fuck you doing just popping up like this?" He hopped the fence and came up the steps. He took his key and opened the front door.

She stepped inside and shook her umbrella out on the porch. "I didn't think I needed an invitation. Besides, Makaroni told me to check in with you a long time ago. I just

took my time doing it. But I'm here now. Deal with it." She sat the umbrella upright and took her coat off.

Stevo closed the door and pulled his beater off. He wrung it out over the sink. Then, he tossed it in the trash. "Man, I don't know why Makaroni got you checking in on me. Everything good over here." He grabbed a dry towel and wiped his body off. Then, he sat across from Montana. He could smell her from where he sat. "Damn, you smell good. Tell the truth, you ain't come over here for Makaroni, did you? You came over here so I can give you some of his pipe." He laughed.

"Yeah,right." Montana dismissed him and bruised his ego. "For real though, how is my brother's operations doing?"

"They are thriving. He done made a few hundred thousand since he been gone. That's all you need to know. Now back to us. You saying I can't get none of that pussy no more? Fa real? You do know what I'm out here doing in these streets, don't you?" He scooted to the edge of the couch. He eyed her thighs. They looked as if they wanted to bust out of her Fendi jeans. The rainwater made them that much tighter. Stevo imagined what it felt like to fuck her the last time they had been together. He felt himself getting aroused. She looked so good to him with her curly hair, and freshly done nails. The baby hairs along her edges were sexy as well to him. He wanted some of Montana.

"Boy. Don't nobody care what you out here doing. I ain't one of those sack chasing ass bum bitches. I get my own money. I'm making my own way. You betta check up on me."

Stevo slid beside her on the couch. "Fuck all dat. You in my shit. If I wanna fuck somethin right now, then that's what we finna do. I don't give a fuck who you thank you is. You still 'ol regular ass Montana to me. Fuck yo money."

Montana got up and sat in his previous seat. She crossed her thick thighs. "That's how I feel about yo shit. Fuck yo money, too. Now, what's good with Keaira?"

Stevo shrugged his shoulder. "I don't know. I ain't heard from her in a minute. I think she skipped town. She might of went back to Madison."

"Madison? Boy she ain't went back to no boring ass Madison, Wisconsin. You gotta come betta than that." Montana encouraged.

Stevo stood up. "I don't know, and I don't give a fuck. Wherever she at, I hope she stay. I ain't had this much peace since before I got her ass pregnant. So, fuck her. Why you asking so many questions about Keaira anyway? Since when did y'all become so cool?"

"What about Kandace? You heard from her?" Montana watched him closely.

Stevo froze. "Say, shorty? Why you asking me all these weird ass questions?" He mugged her.

Montana eyed the gun in his waistband. She looked up from it into his menacing eyes. "When was the last time you spoke to Kandace?"

"Why, bitch? Who the fuck you think you is to be all up in my shit asking me a bunch of questions?" He felt himself getting angry. He wondered if Montana was wearing a wire.

"You selling pussy?" She asked. "Young girls and shit?"

Now, he was convinced that she was working with the police. He cleared the distance between them and ripped open her shirt. In one yank, her bra came off next. He searched for a wire while she swung at him. "Bitch, you working wit' dem people?"

Montana pushed him off of her and held her titties. "You got me fucked up, Stevo. That rat shit ain't in my blood nigga." She ran over and grabbed her coat, then zipped it up.

"Den why the fuck you asking me all of these crazy questions? This shit seem odd." He stepped into her face. She could smell his stale breath. The scent was Doublemint, and alcohol.

"I picked Kandace up a few days ago. She was telling me some shit that I don't know whether to believe it or not. It's pretty farfetched, but then again, I gotta remember how crazy you are."

"Fuck she tell you?" He snapped.

"That you killed Keaira, and some girl named Carmen. That ring any bells?" Montana didn't know why she was spilling the beans. She guessed that Stevo's reactions would tell her everything she needed to know. What she didn't bank on was the fact that Stevo was a sociopath. He knew how to shield certain emotions because he barely had any.

"I know her lil' ass ain't over there telling you that bullshit." He laughed. "She just mad cause I spanked her. Did you know that she was tooting heroin?"

Montana nodded. "Yep, she said that you got her hooked on it. Not only is she tooting it, but she shooting that shit, too. She had a whole bunch of it. She say she took it from you before she ran away."

Stevo laughed again. "Check this out, Montana. How about we both go approach her lil' ass. I guarantee she won't be telling you all of these lies if I was standing right there. I'll bet you a grand." He prayed that she took the bait. He swore that as soon as he saw Kandace that he was blowing her head off of her shoulders with no mercy.

"Was you fucking her?" Montana asked ignoring his wager.

"What?"

"You heard me. Was you fucking that lil' girl? She described yo dick to me to the tee. I don't think she lying. I knew

168

you was one of them types." She crossed her arms in front of her.

"Fuck I look like messing wit' a lil' girl? You got me fucked up, shorty. I don't get down like that." He lied.

"Oh, n'all?" Montana antagonized him.

"Bitch, n'all."

She pointed down the hall. "You wanna explain that?"

Sasha stood in the doorway of the hallway in just a pair of white boy shorts. "Daddy, I'm sick. I need a fix. Please." She felt like she was close to vomiting.

Stevo grabbed Montana by the throat and picked her up in the air. He slammed her to the floor so hard that he knocked the wind out of her. She bit on her cheek. He stuffed the gun into her mouth so far that she gagged over the barrel. "Now, you listen to me Montana and you listen good; You finna take me to where this bitch is, or I'm gon' cut off each one of yo limbs until you do. Do you understand me? Nod your head if you do?"

Montana nodded. She felt like at least two of her ribs were broken. She felt tears coming down her eyes. She wished that Makaroni was beside her. She would've never had to experience such pain and agony.

Stevo looked into Montana's face with hatred. He didn't care what happened between him and Kandace, he had plans on killing Montana no matter what. She knew way too much. He could always blame the murder on Stacy and his goons. Yeah, she had to go. He thought. "Bitch, let's go." He yanked her up by her hair. "Sasha, go get me a shirt, and grab my guns from the dresser. I'll get you a fix in the car."

"Okay, daddy." She hurried off to follow his commands.

***

169

Cassidy stepped into Maisey's house and saw that all of the lights were out. She glanced at her phone and read 9:01pm. She thought that seemed odd. Both Maisey and Seth were usually roaming around the house until at least eleven at night. She kicked off her shoes, and stacked them by the door. She carried them in her hands on the way to her room when she saw a figure standing in the darkness of the living room. She jumped back.

Seth reached out for her. "Baby, don't be alarmed."

Cassidy figured out that it was him and cursed under her breath. "Seth? What is the matter with you? Why are you standing around in the dark?"

"I got this special evening planned for us. I been waiting for you to get here for a whole two hours?" He informed her.

"I'm too tired for all of that." She walked out of the front room into the living room. There the table was decorated with candles. There were two empty plates that Seth had set for them. She stopped in her tracks. "What's all of this?" she asked in awe.

Seth came up behind her and slid his arms around her waist. "I just wanted to do something special for you, baby." He turned her around until she was facing him.

Cassidy's eyes adjusted to the darkness with help from the candles. She looked into his handsome bearded face and felt a twinge of guilt for stepping out on him with Makaroni.

"Don't you still love me, Cassidy? I mean after all we been through." He needed any form of an emotional response from her. He didn't want to do what he was going to do. But he felt like he had no choice. "Please, just tell me you love me." He begged.

Cassidy winced. "Seth, I can't do this right now. I just can't." She walked away from him.

Seth shook his head. He felt torn. He pulled the .380 out of his pockets and cocked it. "I know you cheating on me with Makaroni, Cassidy. I know you been sleeping with that boy! I can't take this shit no more!" He aimed and cocked the hammer of his gun.

*　*　*

Phoenix slowly opened the door to his Chevy Tahoe. He and three of his closest day ones slipped out of the truck and dropped low to the ground. They ran full speed until they got to the gate that separated Jahliya's mansion from the outside world. Once there, they hopped the gate and ran across the lawn. They were dressed in all black from ski mask to black Navy boots. Each man was equipped with a Military edition assault rifles and six grenades. They made haste across the lawn. When they got outside of Jahliya's mansion, they each took a side. One man took the front. Another the back. One took the east side. Another the west. Phoenix stood at the front of the mansion. He took a step back and pulled the first pin of his grenade with his teeth. He threw it through the glass window and followed that one with another one. The grenades broke through the windows and rolled across Jahliya's white floor. In eight seconds, they exploded. Phoenix's men took that as their cue to do the same. They hoisted their grenades into the window and ran away from the mansion. The palace exploded. The men waited for the occupants to run out of the mansion so they could gun them down with armor piercing bullets. Phoenix refused to lose. Nothing or nobody would stand in the way of him inheriting the Rebirth and its throne.

To Be Continued...
Drug Lords 3

171

Ghost

Coming Soon

Submission Guideline

Submit the first three chapters of your completed manuscript to ldpsubmissions@gmail.com, subject line: Your book's title. The manuscript must be in a .doc file and sent as an attachment. Document should be in Times New Roman, double spaced and in size 12 font. Also, provide your synopsis and full contact information. If sending multiple submissions, they must each be in a separate email.

Have a story but no way to send it electronically? You can still submit to LDP/Ca$h Presents. Send in the first three chapters, written or typed, of your completed manuscript to:

LDP: Submissions Dept
Po Box 870494
Mesquite, Tx 75187

DO NOT send original manuscript. Must be a duplicate.

Provide your synopsis and a cover letter containing your full contact information.

Thanks for considering LDP and Ca$h Presents.

<u>Coming Soon from Lock Down Publications/Ca$h Presents</u>

BOW DOWN TO MY GANGSTA

By **Ca$h**

TORN BETWEEN TWO

By **Coffee**

BLOOD STAINS OF A SHOTTA **III**

By **Jamaica**

STEADY MOBBIN **III**

By **Marcellus Allen**

BLOOD OF A BOSS **VI**

SHADOWS OF THE GAME II

By **Askari**

LOYAL TO THE GAME **IV**

By **T.J. & Jelissa**

A DOPEBOY'S PRAYER II

By **Eddie "Wolf" Lee**

IF LOVING YOU IS WRONG... **III**

By **Jelissa**

TRUE SAVAGE **VII**

MIDNIGHT CARTEL

DOPE BOY MAGIC II

By **Chris Green**

BLAST FOR ME **III**

DUFFLE BAG CARTEL **IV**

HEARTLESS GOON **IV**

A SAVAGE DOPEBOY II

DRUG LORDS III

By **Ghost**

A HUSTLER'S DECEIT III

KILL ZONE **II**

BAE BELONGS TO ME III

SOUL OF A MONSTER III

By **Aryanna**

THE COST OF LOYALTY **III**

By **Kweli**

THE SAVAGE LIFE III

By **J-Blunt**

KING OF NEW YORK V

COKE KINGS IV

BORN HEARTLESS III

By **T.J. Edwards**

GORILLAZ IN THE BAY V

De'Kari

THE STREETS ARE CALLING II

Duquie Wilson

KINGPIN KILLAZ IV

STREET KINGS III

PAID IN BLOOD III

CARTEL KILLAZ IV

Hood Rich

SINS OF A HUSTLA II

ASAD

TRIGGADALE III

Ghost

Elijah R. Freeman
KINGZ OF THE GAME V
Playa Ray
SLAUGHTER GANG IV
RUTHLESS HEART II
By Willie Slaughter
THE HEART OF A SAVAGE II
By Jibril Williams
FUK SHYT II
By Blakk Diamond
THE DOPEMAN'S BODYGAURD II
By Tranay Adams
TRAP GOD II
By Troublesome
YAYO II
A SHOOTER'S AMBITION II
By S. Allen
GHOST MOB
Stilloan Robinson
KINGPIN DREAMS II
By Paper Boi Rari
CREAM
By Yolanda Moore
SON OF A DOPE FIEND II
By Renta
FOREVER GANGSTA II
By Adrian Dulan

176

LOYALTY AIN'T PROMISED

By Keith Williams

THE PRICE YOU PAY FOR LOVE II

By Destiny Skai

THE LIFE OF A HOOD STAR

By Rashia Wilson

TOE TAGZ II

By Ah'Million

Available Now

RESTRAINING ORDER **I & II**

By **CA$H & Coffee**

LOVE KNOWS NO BOUNDARIES **I II & III**

By **Coffee**

RAISED AS A GOON I, II, III & IV

BRED BY THE SLUMS I, II, III

BLAST FOR ME I & II

ROTTEN TO THE CORE I II III

A BRONX TALE I, II, III

DUFFEL BAG CARTEL I II III

HEARTLESS GOON

A SAVAGE DOPEBOY

HEARTLESS GOON I II III

DRUG LORDS I II

By **Ghost**

LAY IT DOWN **I & II**

Ghost

LAST OF A DYING BREED

BLOOD STAINS OF A SHOTTA I & II

By **Jamaica**

LOYAL TO THE GAME

LOYAL TO THE GAME II

LOYAL TO THE GAME III

LIFE OF SIN I, II III

By **TJ & Jelissa**

BLOODY COMMAS I & II

SKI MASK CARTEL I II & III

KING OF NEW YORK I II,III IV

RISE TO POWER I II III

COKE KINGS I II III

BORN HEARTLESS I II

By **T.J. Edwards**

IF LOVING HIM IS WRONG…I & II

LOVE ME EVEN WHEN IT HURTS I II III

By **Jelissa**

WHEN THE STREETS CLAP BACK I & II III

By **Jibril Williams**

A DISTINGUISHED THUG STOLE MY HEART I II & III

LOVE SHOULDN'T HURT I II III IV

RENEGADE BOYS I II III IV

By **Meesha**

A GANGSTER'S CODE I &, II III

A GANGSTER'S SYN I II III

THE SAVAGE LIFE I II

Drug Lords 2

By J-Blunt

PUSH IT TO THE LIMIT

By **Bre' Hayes**

BLOOD OF A BOSS **I, II, III, IV, V**

SHADOWS OF THE GAME

By **Askari**

THE STREETS BLEED MURDER **I, II & III**

THE HEART OF A GANGSTA I II& III

By **Jerry Jackson**

CUM FOR ME

CUM FOR ME 2

CUM FOR ME 3

CUM FOR ME 4

CUM FOR ME 5

An **LDP Erotica Collaboration**

BRIDE OF A HUSTLA **I II & II**

THE FETTI GIRLS **I, II& III**

CORRUPTED BY A GANGSTA I, II III, IV

BLINDED BY HIS LOVE

THE PRICE YOU PAY FOR LOVE

By **Destiny Skai**

WHEN A GOOD GIRL GOES BAD

By **Adrienne**

THE COST OF LOYALTY I II

By **Kweli**

A GANGSTER'S REVENGE **I II III & IV**

THE BOSS MAN'S DAUGHTERS

Ghost

THE BOSS MAN'S DAUGHTERS II
THE BOSSMAN'S DAUGHTERS III
THE BOSSMAN'S DAUGHTERS IV
THE BOSS MAN'S DAUGHTERS **V**
A SAVAGE LOVE **I & II**
BAE BELONGS TO ME I II
A HUSTLER'S DECEIT I, II, III
WHAT BAD BITCHES DO I, II, III
SOUL OF A MONSTER I II
KILL ZONE
By **Aryanna**
A KINGPIN'S AMBITON
A KINGPIN'S AMBITION **II**
I MURDER FOR THE DOUGH
By **Ambitious**
TRUE SAVAGE
TRUE SAVAGE II
TRUE SAVAGE **III**
TRUE SAVAGE **IV**
TRUE SAVAGE **V**
TRUE SAVAGE **VI**
DOPE BOY MAGIC
MIDNIGHT CARTEL
By **Chris Green**
A DOPEBOY'S PRAYER
By **Eddie "Wolf" Lee**
THE KING CARTEL **I, II & III**

Drug Lords 2

By **Frank Gresham**

THESE NIGGAS AIN'T LOYAL **I, II & III**

By **Nikki Tee**

GANGSTA SHYT **I II &III**

By **CATO**

THE ULTIMATE BETRAYAL

By **Phoenix**

BOSS'N UP **I , II & III**

By **Royal Nicole**

I LOVE YOU TO DEATH

By Destiny J

I RIDE FOR MY HITTA

I STILL RIDE FOR MY HITTA

By **Misty Holt**

LOVE & CHASIN' PAPER

By **Qay Crockett**

TO DIE IN VAIN

SINS OF A HUSTLA

By **ASAD**

BROOKLYN HUSTLAZ

By **Boogsy Morina**

BROOKLYN ON LOCK I & II

By **Sonovia**

GANGSTA CITY

By **Teddy Duke**

A DRUG KING AND HIS DIAMOND I & II III

A DOPEMAN'S RICHES

Ghost

HER MAN, MINE'S TOO I, II

CASH MONEY HO'S

By Nicole Goosby

TRAPHOUSE KING **I II & III**

KINGPIN KILLAZ I II III

STREET KINGS I II

PAID IN BLOOD **I II**

CARTEL KILLAZ I II III

By **Hood Rich**

LIPSTICK KILLAH **I, II, III**

CRIME OF PASSION I II & III

By **Mimi**

STEADY MOBBN' **I, II, III**

By **Marcellus Allen**

WHO SHOT YA **I, II, III**

SON OF A DOPE FIEND

Renta

GORILLAZ IN THE BAY **I II III IV**

DE'KARI

TRIGGADALE I II

Elijah R. Freeman

GOD BLESS THE TRAPPERS I, II, III

THESE SCANDALOUS STREETS I, II, III

FEAR MY GANGSTA I, II, III

THESE STREETS DON'T LOVE NOBODY I, II

BURY ME A G I, II, III, IV, V

A GANGSTA'S EMPIRE I, II, III, IV

Drug Lords 2

THE DOPEMAN'S BODYGAURD

Tranay Adams

THE STREETS ARE CALLING

Duquie Wilson

MARRIED TO A BOSS... I II III

By Destiny Skai & Chris Green

KINGZ OF THE GAME I II III IV

Playa Ray

SLAUGHTER GANG I II III

RUTHLESS HEART

By Willie Slaughter

THE HEART OF A SAVAGE

By Jibril Williams

FUK SHYT

By Blakk Diamond

DON'T F#CK WITH MY HEART I II

By Linnea

ADDICTED TO THE DRAMA I II III

By Jamila

YAYO

A SHOOTER'S AMBITION

By S. Allen

TRAP GOD

By Troublesome

FOREVER GANGSTA

By Adrian Dulan

TOE TAGZ

Ghost

By Ah'Million
KINGPIN DREAMS
By Paper Boi Rari

BOOKS BY LDP'S CEO, CA$H

TRUST IN NO MAN

TRUST IN NO MAN 2

TRUST IN NO MAN 3

BONDED BY BLOOD

SHORTY GOT A THUG

THUGS CRY

THUGS CRY 2

THUGS CRY 3

TRUST NO BITCH

TRUST NO BITCH 2

TRUST NO BITCH 3

TIL MY CASKET DROPS

RESTRAINING ORDER

RESTRAINING ORDER 2

IN LOVE WITH A CONVICT

Coming Soon

BONDED BY BLOOD 2

BOW DOWN TO MY GANGSTA

Ghost

Printed in the USA
CPSIA information can be obtained
at www.ICGtesting.com
CBHW051226200124
3632CB00011B/796